THE HARBINGER OF DOOM

Thomas Cartwright thought the terrible fate which had dogged him for so many years had finally found another target. However, this was not so, for his life became a tangled web of violence, deceit and treachery. When in a dream he met his late wife and children below Watersmeet, then expounded his fantasies to Maria, he almost lost the love of this wonderful woman, who had been his lover and companion for more than half a century. The revellations made known to him at Watersmeet were as a message from the grave, yet if it hadn't been for Maria, Thomas may not have recovered from that terrible blow.

Books by Edward Hewitt
Published by The House of Ulverscroft:

THE CARTWRIGHT SAGA:
WHERE WATERS MEET VOL. I

EDWARD HEWITT

THE HARBINGER OF DOOM

The Cartwright Saga
Volume Two

Complete and Unabridged

ULVERSCROFT
Leicester

First published in Great Britain in 1997

First Large Print Edition
published 2000

The moral right of the author has been asserted

British Library CIP Data

Hewitt, Edward
    The harbinger of doom.—Large print ed.—
(The Cartwright saga; v. 2)
Ulverscroft large print series: romance
1. Love stories
2. Large type books
I. Title
823.9′14 [F]

ISBN 0–7089–4168–0

Published by
F. A. Thorpe (Publishing) Ltd.
Anstey, Leicestershire
Set by Words & Graphics Ltd.
Anstey, Leicestershire
Printed and bound in Great Britain by
T. J. International Ltd., Padstow, Cornwall

This book is printed on acid-free paper

Prologue

The Gold Fields
New South Wales
Australia

Summer 1860

A well built, thick set man in his mid-thirties was sitting alone, at a table in the corner of a ramshackle canteen, situated in the gold fields of New South Wales.

He was nursing a glass of warm beer in one hand, while idly turning the pages of a tattered copy of the *Sydney Times* with the other, when suddenly his eyes became riveted on a small paragraph halfway down the central column on the third page:

> Will Charles Butlin, late of Kingston-upon-Hull please contact Hodge, Beadle & Hodge, Solicitors of Harbour Street, Sydney. Where he will learn something to his advantage.

Charlie read the words again. He couldn't believe his eyes, and yet there could be

1

no other Charles Butlin from Hull, here in Australia.

When he was a boy of twelve, his father had taken him down to the docks late one night, given the captain a small bag of sovereigns, and put Charlie on board this ship which was due to sail on the morning tide, bound for Australia.

He had been taken below to the quarters of the ship's carpenter, Sam Wright, an old sea dog, who had also sailed from Hull to Australia, some forty years before. This was Sam's last voyage, for he was retiring from the sea, but still intended to continue working in the shipyards near his home in Sydney.

Sam had taken an instant liking to the sturdy young lad who had been thrust upon him and, during the long sea voyage, they became firm friends. So much so that ultimately Sam had decided to take on the youngster as an apprentice.

Mrs Wright, a homely kind hearted soul, had never been blessed with children of her own, and when Sam suggested taking on the fostering of young Charles, she was a little dubious at first. However, with the aid of the lad's cheeky grin, and his apparent willingness to work and run errands for his wife, Sam finally persuaded her to give the boy a chance.

So Charlie had stayed on with the ship's carpenter and his wife, and had made a good life for himself. Sam was a very good tradesman and Charlie proved to be an apt pupil. Consequently between them they had built up quite a sound business, working not only on ships, but on shops and houses too.

Over the years Sam had made his foster son a partner and, in the late summer of eighteen fifty, had announced his retirement, handing over the reins of authority to Charles.

With four other tradesmen and two apprentices, Charlie continued to prosper, for this was a new and vibrant country, and for anyone who was young, fit and willing to work, the rewards were there for the taking.

For the next three years, it seemed as though the continual flow of orders and contracts would never cease. Then, quite suddenly, in the year eighteen fifty three, something happened which was to change the lives of Australians for many generations to come. It was as if a shock wave had hit the whole Continent.

Gold had been discovered!

Men left the factories, the shipyards, the sheep stations and the building sites, in their thousands. One week Charlie and his men were working flat out and the next he was alone.

Everyone seemed to have gold fever, so Charlie, after giving the matter some considerable thought, and having sought Sam's blessing, had decided to join in this quest for the soft yellow metal, which has lured more men to death than to riches since the beginning of time.

Seven years had passed since the first gold had been discovered, and during that time Charlie had amassed for himself, quite a respectable fortune. At the last count, several weeks ago, he had the sum of seventy thousand pounds in his bank account and had been seriously considering giving up this eternal quest for more.

He had actually been thinking of returning to the old country and home, when he first began turning the pages of this old newspaper. Reading the paragraph once again, his mind was made up and, deftly removing it from the page, he carefully folded the small piece of paper and placed it in his wallet.

★ ★ ★

If any of Charlie Butlin's gold mining friends had seen him striding down Harbour Street

4

three weeks later, they would never have recognised him. Gone was the beard, the long matted hair, the ragged shirt, filthy corduroys and worn out boots. In their place was a well dressed, clean shaven man, in a good fitting tweed suit, and highly polished brown boots.

He was walking along, scrutinising the names above all the shops and offices, and beginning to perspire a little in the warm morning sun, when at last he found what he was looking for: Hodge, Beadle & Hodge, Solicitors.

Stepping briskly up the steps and through the main door, he was accosted by a bespectacled, pimply youth. 'What is your business, sir?' asked the pimply one.

'I wish to see one of your Hodges,' replied Charlie.

'One of our Hodges? Do you mean Mr Hodge?' the youth asked, his nose in the air.

Charlie grabbed him by his shirt front. 'Now look, don't muck me about son, I've come too damned far to take any cheek from the likes of you. Take me to see somebody. Quick!' Charlie thought the young man was going to faint as he released him.

'Please follow me sir,' he said tremulously.

He was taken upstairs and into a large

musty smelling office, the walls of which were lined with dusty books and files. Sitting behind a huge knee-hole desk, which was littered with papers and legal looking documents, sat a large, balding, fat man with tiny, pig-like eyes, and a pair of thick bottle bottom spectacles perched on the end of his nose.

The man looked up from whatever he had been doing. 'Ah, good morning. Take off your coat.'

Charlie, looking baffled, sat down on the chair placed his side of the desk. 'Good morning. I'm not wearing a coat.'

Mr Hodge, for Charlie had correctly assumed this must be one of the Hodges, peered intently at his client. 'Ah, good, I see you have already taken it off. Well, sit down man. Now, what is your name and business?'

'My name sir, is Charles Butlin, and my business is this,' said Charlie, as he withdrew from his wallet the small paragraph he had removed from the newspaper and passed it to the solicitor.

The man lifted it to within two inches of his nose, studied the small missive carefully, and then handed it back. 'What does it say?' he asked.

'Some solicitor he is,' thought Charlie.

'The silly fat old sod can't see. That must be why he told me to take off my coat when I wasn't wearing one, and why he told me to sit down when I already had.' Aloud, he read out the contents of the newspaper clipping.

Mr Hodge leaned forward, placed his elbows on the desk and steepled his fat fingers, peering over them at Charlie, as if trying to recognise him. 'And I suppose you sir, are about to try and persuade me that your name in Charles Butlin.'

'By, you're quick. Of course it is. That's why I'm here man!' Charlie was quickly losing what little patience he had.

'Yes yes, I understand, but have you any identification? Can you prove you are Charles Butlin?'

'Damn it, man! I've already told you who I am, what more do you want?'

At that moment they were interrupted by a knock on the door, and a small dapper man walked in carrying a black bag, accompanied by the pimply youth. 'Excuse me Mr Hodge, but Dr Palsey is here for his ten thirty appointment.'

Charlie quickly turned. 'Thank God you're here doc. Will you please tell this silly old fool who I am?'

For a moment the doctor stared at the well dressed stranger before him, and then

7

a light of recognition dawned in his eyes. Stepping forward, his hand outstretched, he exclaimed. 'Why bless my soul. I do believe you are Charles Butlin. My word, you have filled out somewhat since I last saw you.'

They shook hands, then the doctor's countenance saddened. 'Has Hodge told you about Sam?'

Charlie gave the solicitor a withering look. 'He hasn't told me a damn thing, doc. He wouldn't even believe I was me.'

On a less serious occasion, Dr Palsey would have smiled at Charlie's use of the Queen's English. Now however, he looked up at him and said kindly. 'Old Sam died about a year ago Charlie, and the next day his wife followed him.'

Charlie gripped the back of his chair, and then sat down. He didn't speak, but just sat there, his leathery skin a shade paler, beneath its tan of years in the fierce Australian sun.

The doctor leaned towards Hodge. 'Have you any whisky?' he asked quietly. Without replying, the solicitor slid open a drawer in his desk, and produced a bottle of whisky and a glass. Pouring out a good measure, he handed it to Charlie, who accepted the drink gratefully, disposing of it in one gulp.

For a moment there was silence in the room, as Charlie gently rolled the empty glass around between his thick callused fingers. Slowly, the fiery liquid began to take effect, as it coursed through his veins.

Suddenly he leapt to his feet. 'Do you have another couple of glasses, Hodge?' he demanded belligerently. Alarmed by the tone and manner of this stranger, Hodge silently produced two more glasses and placed them upon his desk.

Charlie picked up the bottle, and poured a good stiff measure into all three glasses, handing one each to his companions, and picking up the third one himself.

The window immediately behind Hodge's desk, overlooked the sea and the docks. Charlie, walking behind the desk, said with a wave of his hand. 'Out there is the sea that Sam loved so much, and down there is the place he loved to work. Will you two gentlemen drink a toast with me, to Sam and his wife, wherever they may be?'

The solicitor raised his bulk from his chair, and the doctor came and stood beside them, as these three men, worlds apart in their separate professions, yet all close friends of Sam and his wife when they were alive, raised their glasses and said in unison, 'To Sam and his wife.'

As though controlled by some invisible puppeteer, they stood for a moment in

9

silence after draining their glasses then, as one man, they turned away from the window.

'Now, Mr Hodge, what is this I'm going to hear to my advantage?' asked Charlie quietly.

The plump solicitor wobbled across his office to the stacks of files. With his nose almost touching the third shelf from the bottom, he peered closely at each file as he moved along, until finally he found the one bearing Sam Wright's name. Pulling out the file, he carried it over to the window, where the light was much stronger, and flipping open the file he withdrew a long brown envelope sealed with a large blob of sealing wax.

Carefully scrutinising the name on the envelope, after once more adjusting his spectacles, Hodge emitted an audible sigh of relief, as a magician might, after producing a rabbit out of a hat for the first time.

'There you are Mr Charles Butlin. This is for you sir,' said the solicitor triumphantly, as he handed over the envelope.

Charlie broke the seal with his thick fingers, and emptied the contents on Hodge's desk. Two important looking documents spilled out, followed by another envelope and a bunch of keys. Charlie immediately recognised the keys as those which fit Sam's house and workshop, then tearing open the second envelope, he removed a letter and began to read.

Suddenly, he shattered the peace and quiet of Hodge's dusty domain, with an explosive epithet. 'Well damn me!' he shouted. 'Old Sam has left me the whole damned lot! His house, his workshop and everything. Including all his tools and furniture. He has also left me the deeds to five hundred acres of land on the outskirts of town, and three thousand pounds in the bank!'

Charlie was so overcome, he sat down again, and after replacing the letter in its envelope, he picked up the two documents. One was the deeds for his five hundred acres of land, and the other for his house and workshop.

Dr Palsey slapped him on the back. 'Well done Charlie,' he beamed. 'You are a man of property now and considerable wealth. What are you going to do, start the old firm up again?'

Charlie was quiet for a long moment. Then, standing up, he withdrew a new leather cigar case from his pocket, and offered a cigar to each of his companions. By the time the doctor and Hodge had cut off the ends of their cigars, and were obviously enjoying the aromatic flavour to their mutual satisfaction, Charlie had decided to tell them of his plans.

'No gentlemen. I am not going to start up the old firm. As a matter of fact, I may never work again! You see I had a bit of luck in the gold fields, and already had a few thousand tucked away before today.'

His two listeners gave gasps of astonishment. Hodge began to rub his ghastly, fat, sweaty hands together, and beads of perspiration had appeared upon his brow. His thick glasses began to film over, and when he removed them to clean, his little piggy eyes, seemed to shout the word: Avarice!

'Why that is good news, Mr Charles. Very good news indeed,' he said, mopping his glistening brow, and failing completely to hide his inordinate greed. 'You will of course engage us to attend to all your legal matters, including the sale of your property, should you decide to sell?'

Charlie felt nauseated at the sight of this quivering mass of blubber, almost pleading for him to reply in the affirmative. With an unprecedented, yet remarkable and conscious effort of will, he restrained himself from sinking his knotted fist into the man's bulging paunch.

He contemptuously ignored the question, and turned quickly to Dr Palsey. 'Well, I must be going Doc. I have a great many things to attend to now, but I will try and see you again before I leave.'

'Before you leave! But you have only just arrived. Where are you going to Charlie?' asked the doctor, his curiosity getting the better of him.

'Sorry Doc, didn't I tell you? I'm going back to old England as soon as I have sold my inheritance and booked a passage. Good day to you.'

The room was quiet after Charlie had left, and the doctor reflected how fortuitous his timely intervention had been for the obnoxious Hodge. He remembered old Sam telling him on more than one occasion what a short fuse Charlie Butlin had, and he was convinced if he had not arrived promptly for his appointment that morning, the obese figure of Mr Hodge would at that moment be stretched out unconscious on his own office floor. The good doctor, had great difficulty in suppressing a smile, as he relished the thought of that inglorious prospect . . .

As Charlie walked out onto the bright sunlit street, he decided to go and have a look at his recently acquired property. The old place looked just as he remembered it, though he noticed the doors and windows could have done with a lick of paint.

When he had finished his inspection of the house and its contents, Charlie turned his attention to Sam's workshop. Though not normally of a sentimental nature, he couldn't prevent the tears which pricked uncomfortably behind his eyelids, as he fondled some of Sam's favourite tools, and the memories of days long gone came flooding back.

Angrily brushing away the tears with his coat sleeve, and silently cursing himself for being such a sentimental fool, he hurried from the workshop.

As he emerged too quickly from the side gate leading to the street, he collided violently with a man who was just walking past.

'Why the hell don't you look where you're going?' the man snarled.

Charlie grabbed him by the shoulder and spun him round, his arm drawn back ready to deliver a telling blow with his fist to the other's chin. Suddenly he stopped and stared. 'Why, it's Harry Dixon!' he shouted.

The other man looked at him keenly for a moment, and then a look of recognition dawned in his eyes. 'Charlie Butlin. Sorry mate, I didn't recognise you.'

The two men shook hands and embraced each other affectionately, with much back slapping, for Harry had been Charlie's first employee, and the last one to leave during the gold rush. After the first flush of their renewed acquaintance, Charlie stood back and surveyed his old friend. 'By, you look fit Harry. What the devil are you doing wandering around down here?'

'Well, I thought I would just call in to see you and Sam, and to find out if there's any chance of getting my old job back.' He noticed the change in Charlie's demeanour. 'What's up Chas? Old Sam's all right, isn't he?'

'I'm afraid not Harry. You obviously haven't heard. Sam and his wife died within a few hours of each other, about a year ago. I only found out myself this morning.'

Harry was visibly shaken. 'Hell, that is bad news Charlie. Poor old Sam.' Then after a moments silence. 'What did you mean Charlie. You only found out this morning, if they died a year ago?'

Charlie smiled. 'Because I only came back yesterday from New South Wales.'

His friend interrupted him. 'Do you mean you joined the gold rush after all?' asked Harry in surprise. 'I came here this morning hoping to get my old job back, and now I find Sam and his wife have died, and you have only just returned from the gold fields. By the way, did you have any luck Charlie?'

'Yes I did that,' replied Charlie, smiling broadly. 'I made several thousand. Then a few weeks ago, in an old newspaper, I found this.' He produced the clipping and showed it to his companion.

Harry read the crumpled piece of paper and handed it back. 'Fancy finding that, out there in the gold fields. Have you been to see these solicitors Charlie?'

'I certainly have. I called in this morning, and you're not going to believe this Harry, but old Sam has left me the lot.'

'Do you mean the house?'

'I mean everything Harry. The house, yard workshop, his tools, and all the furniture in the house.'

His old friend slapped him on the back. 'Congratulations Charlie. When will you be getting the business started again?'

Charlie could see his friend was happy with this news of his inheritance. Obviously Harry's chief concern was his job prospects. 'I'm sorry Harry, but I'm putting the place up for sale, and returning to England.'

Harry appeared downcast, and he stared at Charlie, as though unable to assimilate the words he had just heard. He remained silent, and then, quite suddenly his features brightened, as a wild idea entered his mind. 'Charlie, have you the keys to this place?' he asked excitedly.

'Of course, but what the hell are you driving at, man?'

Harry laughed. 'Don't worry I'll tell you later. Will you show me round? You see I've never been upstairs, and I've often wondered what it was like.'

Charlie looked up at the sun. 'Hell I'm ready for a drink and a bite to eat, so we can't take too much time. Anyway come on, I'll show you.'

Charlie led his friend on a quick tour of the house, and then across the yard and into the workshop. Harry looked around, checking the tools, the benches, and the stock of timber. He then dusted down one of the benches and sat on it.

His companion was becoming impatient. 'Come on Harry. We can't spend all day here, and you know I'm dying for a drink.'

Ignoring this outburst, Harry continued to sit upon the bench, swinging his legs. 'How much Charlie?' he asked nonchalantly.

Charlie, who had just started for the door, stopped dead in his tracks and spun around. 'How much?' he echoed. 'What the hell are you going on about Harry? How much what?'

'All right Charlie, let's keep it simple. You want to sell this property, I want to buy it. I'll ask you again. How much?'

Charlie walked over to the opposite bench, dusted it off and sat down. He stared at his friend in astonishment. 'Well damn me. You're real serious about this, aren't you Harry?'

'Yes I am. Now I'm going to ask you once more, and don't be thinking of jacking up the price with any fancy goodwill for the business, because there ain't any. I shall have to start completely from scratch. Now, I will ask you for the third and last time Charlie Butlin. How much?'

Charlie could see his old friend and ex-employee was eager to get his hands on the place, but he wasn't worried, for he had worked out exactly how much to ask for the property earlier that morning. 'Well I was going to paint all the woodwork on the outside of the house and workshop, and put a price of three hundred and fifty pounds on it. However if you accept the place as it is, and do all the painting yourself, the price will be reduced to three hundred and twenty five.'

Harry sat for a moment, his brain working overtime, doing some quick mental arithmetic. Then, leaping off the bench, he stepped across to Charlie, his hand outstretched. 'It's a deal,' he said. 'Let's shake on it, then go and have that drink you keep harping on about.'

They shook hands warmly, for Charlie knew his friend to be a very good tradesman and a conscientious, responsible person, and had no qualms about selling his windfall to Harry.

1

Kingston-upon-Hull

Several weeks later, Charlie Butlin alighted from a train in Paragon Station, having travelled up from London, changed trains at Doncaster and thence to Kingston-upon-Hull. He gazed about him in wide eyed amazement for, of course the station was all new to him. In fact there hadn't even been a railway line to the town when he was a boy.

He summoned a porter to help with his luggage and, when they reached the street, the man called a waiting cab. 'Where to sir?' asked the driver, after he and the porter had stowed Charlie's heavy trunks.

Charlie hesitated. He didn't really know. 'Is there still a Town Square?' he asked.

'Yes, sir,' the driver replied.

'Good. Take me to a small quiet inn, just off the square, if you know of one.'

'I certainly do sir. Climb aboard and I'll have you there in no time like.'

His passenger sat back and smiled to himself as he reflected on this odd way the true natives of Hull had of quite often finishing a sentence with the word 'like.' He had never heard it used in this context anywhere else but here in his native town.

Within a few minutes, the cab drew to a halt outside a comfortable looking inn, down a side street just off the square. Charlie stepped down from the cab, carrying a leather case. 'Just let me check to see if they have a vacancy, and then you can find someone to help you with the trunks,' he said to the driver.

He walked through the door into a small hall, where a pretty young wench was sitting behind a desk. 'Good afternoon sir. Will you be needing a room?' she asked, with no trace of a Yorkshire accent.

'Yes please miss, but I have two trunks,' replied Charlie.

The girl brought her palm down smartly upon the knob of a large brass, spring loaded bell. As if by magic, a tall awkward looking youth appeared, through a door off the hall.

'Help the driver with this gentleman's luggage, Steve,' she said curtly, in a very different tone to the one she had used when addressing Charlie. Pulling a large book towards her, she opened it, and looking up, smiled sweetly and asked. 'How long will you be staying, sir?'

Charlie hesitated. 'I don't really know, miss. It might be a week, or I could be here for six months. I have no idea. Anyway, put me down for a week to start with. Do you need any money in advance?'

'No thank you, sir. Will you sign the register please,' she said, turning the book around and pushing it towards Charlie.

He signed with a flourish. She again turned the book, and after reading his name, reached behind her where several keys hung from a rail.

'Here you are, Mr Butlin. Your room is number four, on the first landing at the front.' Thanking her, Charlie picked up his bag and climbed the stairs.

He was pleasantly surprised by the size of his room, and also the furnishings, for it was more of a bed-sitting room, complete with table, chairs and a sofa. The driver and the awkward looking youth came in with his luggage, preventing any further inspection of his new abode. Charlie gave the driver a silver sixpence and the youth a silver threepence, for which they thanked him profusely, touching their caps on the way out.

A few minutes later there was a light tap on his door and the young woman he had seen

23

earlier came in with a jug of hot water. 'I thought you may like to wash and change sir, after your long journey, and before dinner.'

She was obviously a practised flirt, from the two half moons of her nubile breasts spilling over the top of her scanty dress, to the long lingering look she gave him with her dark languorous eyes, promising a flight of sexual fantasy to the realms of Elysium.

For a brief moment, Charlie was tempted, then giving her a slap on her bottom, he ushered her towards the door. 'No thank you love, not just now. Maybe tonight.'

As she flounced out, and was about to close the door, she hesitated for a second, then turned and said pertly. 'Perhaps,' and was gone.

Later, after dinner that night, Charlie went out on the town, calling at various inns for a drink, and by the time he returned, the church clock was chiming eleven thirty. The strong English ale, to which his palate was not yet accustomed, seemed to have rejuvenated his sexual urges, and as he climbed the stairs, he wished he had accepted the blatant offer that wench had made him, when he first arrived.

As he opened his door, he vaguely wondered which room she slept in, and decided to discover that snippet of information tomorrow.

Striking a match, he crossed to the bedside table and lit the candle he had noticed earlier. He undressed slowly, fumbling with his bootlaces and buttons until finally he stood naked, and was about to drop his night-shirt over his head, when suddenly his stomach rebelled at the amount of ale he had consumed that night and he emitted a most horrendous belch.

A muffled female voice, from the direction of the bed said. 'That was not a very nice welcome, sir!'

Charlie cast his night-shirt aside, and flung back the bed covers. She lay there, completely naked. The contours of her superb young body accentuated by the shadows, and the cool white alabaster of her flawless skin, tinted the colour of fresh buttermilk by the flickering candle's yellow flame.

He stood transfixed, drinking her in, and momentarily stunned by the sheer beauty of her. But only momentarily, for Charlie, never being one to look a gift horse in the mouth, quickly rose to the occasion, and literally leapt upon her.

A few seconds later it was over, and he was lying beside her. 'My God!' she gasped. 'What happened? Where have you been?

Living in a monastery for the last couple of years?'

For several minutes Charlie lay panting and perspiring, bereft of all speech by his unaccustomed exertions. Her voice had sounded faint and far away, due to the incessant pounding in his ears. Eventually, however, it subsided, and he managed to regain a little of his normal composure.

'No love. Not in a monastery, but out in the bush in Australia!' he replied, feeling rather ashamed of himself. 'And it wasn't just for a couple of years. I was there for seven,' he added lamely.

Her toes curled and she tingled with anticipatory excitement, as she smiled to herself and thought of the long night ahead. Seven years, he had said. By, he must be hungry for love, and for the rest of this night, he was all hers!

'What is your first name Mr Butlin, I can't keep calling you sir. Well not in bed anyway. Mine's Lucy.'

'Charlie,' he replied. 'Lucy, yes, I rather like that.'

'Shall we try again, Charlie?' she asked softly, as he responded to her practised touch. 'Only this time, please try and be a little more gentle with me. Before, you were like a bull at a gate.'

26

'Aren't you worried about getting pregnant Lucy,' he asked, as he caressed her.

She laughed. 'No, don't you worry about me Charlie Butlin. I have played before you know.'

He was to remember that last remark of hers, and reflect upon it as he rolled off her after the fourth time of coupling within the space of an hour. He lay completely drained and utterly exhausted, oblivious of the fact that Lucy was once again trying to persuade him to show at least a little interest, in her undoubted charms.

When at last she realised her cause was hopeless, and there would be no further response from Charlie that night, she drove her small fists into her pillow, and said aloud. 'Damn you, Charlie Butlin. You're pathetic, just like all men. You talk about nothing else all day, and then when you get the chance, you fall off and go straight to sleep.'

Charlie awoke to the sun streaming through his open curtains. He lay for a while trying to recollect his thoughts, and wondering why he felt so tired after a night's sleep. Then he remembered. He put out his hand to touch her, but her side of the bed was empty. She had gone.

He leapt from the bed, apparently far too quickly, for his head was spinning.

Remembering his drinking spree of the previous evening, he silently cursed the strength of this English ale, and gave himself a quick wash in cold water.

Charlie was blessed with a rugged constitution, and by the time he had finished dressing, he was rejuvenated and back to his old form. Apart from a slight discoloration beneath his eyes, all signs of his weariness from the previous night's erotic exertions had disappeared.

At that moment the breakfast gong sounded, reverberating around the old walls of the small inn, and Charlie realised how hungry he was.

In two strides he was across the room, through the door and bounding down the stairs. She was sitting in her normal position behind the desk. 'Good morning, Mr Butlin,' she greeted him politely, then added in an aside. 'I see you regained consciousness.'

Charlie was thwarted of giving a reply, by the presence of other guests passing through the hall on their way to breakfast. He noticed with a certain amount of gratification that his plate, piled high with bacon and eggs, seemed larger than those of his fellow guests, and he smiled lasciviously to himself as he pondered the reason for this.

After breakfast, Charlie set out to try and

locate his father. He went to his old lodgings in Dagger Lane, but the house had been taken over by some younger people, and he was on the point of leaving, when an old man came forward. 'I couldn't help but hear your conversation like,' he said. 'I knew your father when he lodged here. Come with me.'

Charlie followed the old man to a dingy room at the rear of the house. 'My God! do you live in this hole?' he asked, wrinkling his nose up at the stench and the filthy state of everything. The old man ignored the question, and bending down, dragged out a small trunk from beneath his bed.

'Your father asked me to save this for you, in case he didn't come back one day from work like.'

Charlie stared uncomprehendingly at the man. 'What do you mean, didn't come back? Is he dead?'

The old man sat down upon his filthy bed. 'I don't know son. All I know is that one day he never came back, and I've saved this trunk ever since.'

Charlie tried to be patient. 'How long have you been looking after it?' he asked casually.

The old man sat thinking, as he attempted to work out the number of years. 'About twenty five years I'd say, give or take a year or two.'

'Twenty five years!' shouted Charlie. 'Hell man! Do you mean to tell me my father has been dead for twenty five years, and nobody ever told me?'

The man appeared startled at Charlie's tone and aggressive manner. 'I never said he was dead like. I just said he didn't come home from work,' he whined.

Charlie picked up his trunk and opened the door to leave, then he seemed to have second thoughts, and turning, he flipped the man a florin. 'Sorry old timer. I never meant to have a go at you, and thank you for looking after this for me.' This time he left the room, closing the door behind him.

When he arrived back at the inn, Charlie went straight up to his room. Locking the door, he crossed to the window and placed his trunk upon the table. He tried to open it, but the lid was locked, so drawing the knife, which he always carried in a sheath attached to his belt, he managed to prize it open.

The first things he removed were his father's best jacket and trousers, protected by several sheets of brown paper. The clothes reeked of mothballs, so after shaking them, he hung them on the back of a chair. Then he removed a small canvas bag, tied at the

30

neck by a leather thong. Cutting the leather, he spilled the contents out on to the table.

Drawing up a chair, he sat down and began to examine them. There were several sovereigns, he counted ten in all, three new clay pipes and a brown leather case. Snapping open the case he saw, to his amazement, two George the Third gold five pound coins in absolute mint condition, and a solid silver snuff box.

It was then his eye caught the message on a piece of card, in the lid of the leather case. It was beautifully written in an educated hand. With his heart now beating a little faster, he read the message aloud. 'For Charles, when he attains the age of twenty one years. With Love, Mother.'

For a long while, Charlie Butlin sat and stared at that small piece of card, with mixed emotions. He had never known a mother and, though in his mind he searched as far back over the years as memory would allow, he could not recall at any time ever having had one, only a father.

Finally, he carefully replaced everything the way he had found it, and closed the trunk lid. For Charlie had now decided that his father must be dead, for in the few short years he had known him, he remembered he was never the kind of man who would leave sovereigns lying around in an old tin trunk. Saddened by this thought, yet strengthened in his resolve to find out the truth of his father's death, he pushed any further thought of the mother he had never known from his mind.

That night after dinner, Charlie retired early, and had only been in bed half an hour, when he heard his door open and there she was, pushing back the covers and climbing into bed beside him.

Lucy had a voracious appetite for love, and he knew, no matter how good he was, he would never be able to satisfy her, so he decided from now on, she would have to do her share of the work. Well apparently, Lucy had never previously experienced making love in this manner, and she was completely enraptured with his idea.

So much so in fact, that she came to his room every night, and by the end of the week, though she was well aware he was so much older than herself, she had also become aware of a deep feeling of love and sexual affinity for this dark rugged stranger who had strolled so casually into her life. For she now realised her life style of promiscuity was at an end and that, after Charlie, there could be no other.

On several occasions Charlie endeavoured

to strike up a conversation during these nightly romps, but apparently Lucy had this fixation that, when she was in bed, she was there for two reasons only, and talking certainly was not one of them. Sleep seemed to come a poor second too.

However, he did manage to receive the odd monosyllabic reply to his various questions, thereby discovering that Lucy and her mother, owned and executed the affairs of this inn on their own, for her father had died in the horrific cholera epidemic of eighteen forty nine.

Though Charlie still occupied most of his time wandering the streets of the old town, he savoured his evenings spent in the bar of the inn for, while he was there he could occasionally have a word with Lucy, and now he knew how passionately she loved him, uncharacteristically, albeit unconsciously, he was beginning to reciprocate her feelings.

He was a man who had become accustomed to working with his hands and, though he had enough money to last him for the rest of his life, he was quickly becoming bored with his daily routine.

His enforced idleness during the long sea voyage, coupled with the last three weeks, was proving too much, and inevitably his thoughts turned to shipbuilding and the sea.

The cruel fate which had dogged the Cartwright family for almost two generations, once again reared its ugly formidable head. For this was one of those rare occasions, when a coincidence in real life, is proved to be far greater than any found in fiction.

Charlie was sitting on a bench seat in a corner of the bar room, perusing the jobs vacant columns of the local paper, when a tall lean looking man in his early fifties, walked up to the bar and ordered a pewter mug of ale.

The unusual thing about this was the fact that this was the first time the stranger had ever set foot in this bar. For this was not one of his usual haunts and, as he picked up his drink, Walt turned and surveyed the room. Because of his height, he could see over the heads of most of the customers, and he espied a vacant seat next to a well dressed man reading a newspaper in the corner.

Walt strolled over and seated himself, and though taciturn by nature and of a quiet disposition, he had always found time to pass the time of day with a stranger.

'Evening,' he said as he sat down.

'Evening,' replied the stranger, without raising his eyes from the paper.

Glancing sideways, Walt could just see what the man was reading, and determined not to be put off, thought he would try again. He took a long slow pull on his drink, and after wiping his mouth on the back of his hand. 'Looking for work are you?' he asked in a friendly tone.

For the first time, the stranger looked up, and for a fleeting second, their eyes locked.

'Yes,' he said, unsmiling. 'Why, have you got some for me?'

Walt did not reply. He could not. For when he looked into the stranger's eyes, a shudder had ripped through him. It was as if someone had just walked over his grave.

Though outwardly Walt appeared calm, inwardly he was seething, his brain vainly attempting to shed some light on the reason why the eyes of this stranger should have brought such a sensation of fear to his very soul.

Instinctively he knew he had seen those eyes before, but where and under what circumstances, he could not remember. Thankfully, he noticed the stranger had finished his drink, so picking up his own empty mug, he asked. 'Like another one, mate?'

Charlie looked up, mildly surprised. 'Why yes, thanks,' he replied pushing his mug towards Walt.

When Walt returned to the table with his

two replenished mugs of ale, his companion was just lighting an expensive looking cigar.

As he resumed his seat he noticed lying on the table another cigar waiting for him. 'Thanks,' he said, biting off the end and removing the band. 'By, these are champion, mate.' Then on a sudden impulse, Walt thrust out his hand. 'Walter Ackroyd,' he said, studying the man's eyes.

'Charlie Butlin,' replied Charlie, taking Walt's hand and shaking it warmly.

Walt sat back and enjoyed his cigar for a few minutes, then leaning forward, he said quietly. 'Look Charlie, don't take this the wrong way like, but how come a bloke like you, dressed as you are, can't only afford expensive cigars, but can afford to give one away, when you don't even have a job?'

Charlie, as though resigned to the inevitable, folded his newspaper, picked up his drink and sat back. 'Well, it's like this Walt,' he began. He told Walt of his life in Australia, of how he had learnt his trade as a carpenter, on board ship and ashore, and of how, after having a bit of luck in the gold fields, he had recently returned to England.

He explained, that since his return he was completely bored stiff, with having nothing to do day after day. 'And that Walt, is the reason I'm looking for work in a shipyard,' he finished, as he emptied his sixth mug of ale.

'Right Charlie,' said Walt, for the conversation was flowing more freely now, aided by the liberal lubrication of fine old English ale, for which this particular inn was noted. 'I think I might be able to help you,' he continued. 'I'll have a word with Mr Earnshaw first thing, and then if you come in about eight o'clock, we might have a job for you.'

'Eight o'clock!' slurred Charlie, for he was not yet accustomed to this strong ale. 'Hell's Bells, not as early as that, Walt. I shall have to go out and get fitted up with some working clothes first. If I turn up dressed like this, your gaffer will think I want his flaming job.'

A few heads turned in their direction, at the raucous laughter which greeted this last remark.

After a couple more drinks, and on the understanding that Charlie would turn up at the gates of Earnshaw & Cartwright's shipyard at three o'clock tomorrow afternoon, the two friends parted company, Charlie climbing unsteadily up the stairs to his room and Lucy, and Walt going home to his wife.

Lucy had more than a little trouble with

her lover that night, for all Charlie wanted to do was sleep, and all her feminine charms proved to be of no avail until eventually she had to admit a miserable defeat. However, she did arouse Charlie's interest at six o'clock the following morning, and received more than sufficient recompense to see her through the day.

That afternoon, as the church clock struck three, Charlie walked through the massive gateway leading to Earnshaw and Cartwright's shipyard and, though completely unaware of any sense of danger, followed a predestined path, which eventually would lead to his ultimate self destruction.

Walt was standing beside the night watchman's hut awaiting his arrival. 'By, you look different today, Charlie,' his drinking partner of the previous evening greeted him, as he inspected the new corduroy trousers and coarse working jacket. 'Did you sleep well last night?' he asked as Charlie walked beside him towards the office building.

'Sleep well!' Charlie echoed. 'Hell man, I lay down when I got to my room, fully dressed, boots an'all, and yet when I awoke this morning I was stark naked. Damned if I know what they put in that ale, but it must be mighty powerful stuff.' Walt laughed aloud at his new friend's turn of phrase.

By now they had reached the outer office. Walt led Charlie through, and on to William's private office. The foreman knocked and walked in, followed closely by Charlie.

William was sitting at his desk writing. The two men stood, silently waiting. At last William put down his pen, pushed the ledger to one side and looked up. 'Yes Walt, what is it?' he asked.

Walt stepped forward. 'This is the bloke I was telling you about this morning, sir. You know, the one I met in a bar last night.'

Turning to Charlie, Walt continued. 'Charlie, this is Mr Earnshaw,' and then turning to William. 'Sir. Mr Charles Butlin, ship's carpenter.'

William nodded towards Charlie in acknowledgement. 'All right Walt, leave us now, and come back in half an hour.' He sat back and proceeded to fill his pipe. 'Sit down Charlie,' he said, indicating a chair. When he finally had his pipe going to his satisfaction, he looked at Charlie through a haze of blue tobacco smoke.

'All right Charlie Butlin, tell me one good reason why I should give you this job.'

Charlie leaned forward, and launched himself into telling the story of his past life, beginning with how, at the age of twelve, he had been put on board a ship bound for

Australia, and of how Sam Wright, the ship's carpenter, had taken a fancy to him and had later adopted him, after taking him on as an apprentice.

It was here, for the first time, that William interrupted him. 'Sam Wright, did you say? I knew Sam years ago, when his ship docked here in Hull. Well, if you were apprenticed to Sam, that's good enough for me.'

As he finished speaking, there was a knock on the door and the foreman walked in. 'What do you want Walt?' asked William rather sharply, for he was taking a shine to the rough and ready charisma, which was undoubtedly Charlie's forte, and he certainly knew how to turn it on, when the occasion arose.

'You told me to come back in half an hour, sir,' replied Walt, appearing slightly abashed at the sharpness of his employer's tone.

'Did I Walt? Sorry, I must have forgotten. Anyway, it doesn't matter now, and on your way out tell them in the outer office, I don't want to be disturbed for the rest of the afternoon.'

As Walt closed the office door, William once more turned his attention to Charlie. 'Now let's see. Where were we? Oh yes, I remember, you were telling me about your apprenticeship with Sam Wright.'

Charlie was about to speak, when his prospective employer slid open a drawer in his desk, and produced a bottle of whisky and a couple of glasses. 'Care for a drop, Charlie?' he asked. 'It helps to lubricate the tonsils when talking.'

Charlie accepted the proffered glass, then continued his narration. He told of how he had worked with Sam, and had eventually taken over the business, before joining in the mad rush for gold.

When William had first lit his pipe, and gazed at Charlie through the haze of blue smoke, he'd had a strange feeling he had seen him somewhere before. At the same time he thought he had detected some kind of menace, lurking just below the surface, redolent with evil, emanating from this stranger sitting opposite.

However, on reflection, he realised it was impossible for him to have seen Charlie, if as the man said, he had spent all his adult life in Australia.

He also dismissed his second thought as some figment of his imagination, accentuated by the haze of blue smoke. In later years, there would be those who lived to regret bitterly William Earnshaw ignoring that gut feeling of evil he had experienced when he first looked into the eyes of Charlie Butlin.

William was obviously enjoying these anecdotes of Charlie's life in Australia. So much so, in fact, that a couple of hours had elapsed since he had walked into the office. Looking at his watch, William was astounded to see what time it was, and he interrupted Charlie, who was in the middle of yet another fascinating tale of his life down under.

'You say you worked in houses as well as ships?' he enquired.

'Yes,' replied Charlie, slightly puzzled by the question. He was even more baffled by the next one.

'Where are you living now?'

Charlie told him. 'Why do you want to know? Does this have anything to do with whether I get the job or not?'

William laughed. 'Don't worry about that Charlie, you're already hired.'

He was about to thank him, when William spoke again. 'Do you ride?' he asked.

'Yes, and shoot. I accompanied Sam sometimes on hunting trips into the bush and, before you ask, I also sail and fish. Sam had a fair sized boat, and we often went deep sea fishing at weekends. What are all these questions for anyway?'

His new employer smiled. 'I was just wondering if you would care to come home with me this evening, and maybe stay for the weekend. I'm not in the habit of inviting new employees to stay at Mount Pleasant, or old ones either, but you are slightly different to the majority, having run your own business an'all, plus making a bit of brass prospecting.'

'Anyway you seem like a man's man, and to be honest I would appreciate some male company for a change. My partner Thomas Cartwright, who incidentally is also my son-in-law, is in Europe for another three weeks, negotiating some wine contracts among other things.' He paused for breath.

Suddenly Charlie laughed.

'What the hell are you laughing at?' snapped William, wondering if he had made a joke, and somehow missed it.

'I was just thinking, that must have been quite a speech for you, Mr Earnshaw.'

William chuckled with him. He felt good being in the company of a younger man. 'Yes it was. I don't normally ramble on like that. Anyway, call me William. Now Charlie, are you coming with me?'

Charlie had already decided, after all he had nothing to lose, and a break from his sensual Lucy might be good for them both. 'Yes William, I will come,' he replied. 'I shall have to return to my room and change.

Also to pack a few things. Will you mind waiting?'

'I'll give you half an hour, Charlie, then call round in the trap and pick you up.'

'Right,' said Charlie, rising from his chair. 'See you in half an hour then, and thank you for the job.'

As Charlie left the building, Walt, who had obviously been waiting, fell into step beside him. 'Have you got the job?' he asked.

'Yes, thank you very much, Walt. You're a good mate, I won't forget.' He began to hurry.

'What's the rush Charlie? Where's the damn fire?' shouted the foreman as Charlie began to draw away.

He stopped and waited. 'Sorry Walt, I have to go. Mr Earnshaw is coming to pick me up in half an hour.'

Walt stared at him. 'Pick you up?' he echoed. 'What do you mean, pick you up?'

'I mean,' said Charlie patiently. 'William is calling round with the trap, to take me to his house for the weekend,' and with that remark, Charlie turned on his heel and hurried away, leaving a bemused Walt staring after him.

'Bugger me!' said Walt aloud. 'William, eh! Well bugger me!'

Lucy was sitting beside her desk as Charlie

dashed in. 'Quick, follow me,' he said, as he went bounding up the stairs to his room.

She was only just behind him, as he opened the door and went in. 'Why all the hurry Charlie?' she asked, her eyes shining with anticipation. He had never asked for it during the day. This was going to be wonderful. Her ebullience was short lived however, for when he explained to her what had happened, she clung to him sobbing.

'Oh! Charlie. I cant spend a night alone, not any more. I love you so.' Gently but firmly, he released himself from her embrace, and promised he would return as soon as possible.

Charlie thoroughly enjoyed his ride through the lush English countryside, after the barren wastes of Australia. With his incessant chatter, and stories of his life with Sam, he kept William hugely entertained. So much so, that the massive stone pillars, denoting the entrance to Mount Pleasant, came into view in no time at all.

William's companion gasped, as his employer steered the pony through the gates and down his drive, for the house could just be seen through the tall elms, which flanked it on either side. As they approached, it looked magnificent, nestling in a fold of the hills, splashed by the evening sun.

For the first time during that journey, Charlie was silent, struck dumb by the sheer beauty and size of the place.

'What's up Charlie? Cat got your tongue?' asked William, amused by the expression on the face of his passenger.

'Eh? Oh no, nothing,' stammered Charlie. 'I was just admiring your house. Is this a house William, or is it some kind of palace?'

William laughed as he drew up at the entrance. 'No Charlie, this is no palace, just a decent sized house.'

His two grandchildren came running down the steps to greet him. 'Hello grandpa,' they both cried gaily. They then noticed Charlie and came to a sudden halt, becoming shy and silent.

William jumped down and scooped them up, one in each arm. 'Now children,' he said, as Charlie walked round from the other side of the trap. 'This is Mr Charles Butlin. He is going to stay with us for the weekend. Charlie, meet Beth and Jon.'

Charlie took a small hand in each of his own. 'Hello Beth, Hello Jon,' he said. 'I am very pleased to meet you.'

The two children giggled as they shook hands.

At that moment Kate appeared on the top step, followed closely by Lottie. They came down and were duly introduced to Charlie. Lottie's heart missed a beat as she looked into the stranger's eyes.

However, she decided it must have been a trick of the evening sunlight, which had caused her memory to erupt so, and she immediately banished the impossible thought from her mind.

One of the servants showed Charlie to his room. 'Dinner will be served in the dining room at eight o'clock sir,' the man said, as he was about to leave the room.

'Wait a minute, do we dress for dinner?'

'Yes, it is usual sir,' he replied as he closed the door.

Charlie looked about him. He liked his room, with the slanting rays of the evening sun, coming through the large leaded bow window. Looking out, he could see the Humber and across the river, a great swathe of the flat Lincolnshire landscape.

He unpacked, then washed and changed, and at two minutes to eight was descending the magnificent curved staircase. The servant who had shown him to his room, was just crossing the hall, Charlie took note of which door the man entered and followed him through.

William, Lottie and Kate were already seated when Charlie walked in, and the servant pulled out a chair, sitting him opposite Kate.

His new employer had obviously told them of his exploits in Australia for, all through dinner, the two women continually harassed him with fatuous questions about his life down under.

William could see his guest was becoming bored with the ladies chatter and incessant questioning, so after dinner he suggested that he and Charlie should retire to the billiard room for a quiet chat and a brandy.

When they were comfortably ensconced in a couple of sumptuous leather chairs, with a large brandy each, Charlie produced his inevitable cigar case and handed it to William.

He selected a cigar, sniffed it, then rolled it between a finger and thumb close to his ear. Appearing satisfied, he expertly cut off the end and deftly removed the band then, striking a match, he proceeded to inhale deeply.

'Champion,' said William, holding back his head and gently blowing out perfect rings of blue smoke towards the ceiling. 'I don't think a man has lived, until he has enjoyed the fragrant aroma of a really fine cigar.' Charlie smiled, and wholeheartedly agreed with him.

So, the two men sat on. They smoked their cigars and drank their brandies, and they talked and talked until the early hours. Both of them utterly oblivious of the fact that this stranger to whom William had offered succour, shelter and the hand of friendship, would eventually prove to be a deadly harbinger of doom!

As William and Lottie were dressing that Saturday morning, they were drawn to the open window by loud shrieks of childish laughter coming from below. Looking out, they were both amazed and amused to see Charlie gambolling around on the closely cut grass, being chased by the two children and obviously playing tag. At that moment he allowed Beth to tag him, which resulted in a fresh outburst of excited merriment, as the three of them tumbled in a mass of flying arms and legs upon the damp grass, just as Kate came out to see what all the noise was about.

'Jonathan, Elizabeth! Whatever are you doing to poor Mr Butlin? Get up off that wet grass immediately!' she cried, sternly. They quickly disentangled themselves and staggered to their feet, Charlie looking rather sheepish, and all of them very dishevelled.

'But mama. We didn't hurt him, not really, did we Uncle Charlie?' said the little girl, turning from Kate to look at her new friend.

'No, my dear,' said Charlie, breathing heavily and perspiring profusely from his unusual exertions.

'Please pick me up Uncle Charlie, and give me another piggy back,' cried Jon, clutching Charlie's hand.

'No children. Mr Butlin has had quite enough,' admonished Kate. 'Now come along indoors and have your breakfast.'

As the two children dutifully followed Kate into the house, Lottie turned away from the window and finished dressing. 'Well William, your new man seems to have discovered at least two friends in this household.'

'Ay lass he does that, and if he is half as good as I think he is, he will find one or two more before long,' replied William, as he left the room and went down for breakfast.

When the meal was completed, William escorted his guest on a conducted tour of the house, finally ending in the dining room. 'Now Charlie, I want you to measure the size of this room sometime while you're here, and if you follow me I will show you where the panels are. You see I require you to panel it in oak from floor to ceiling.'

Charlie walked beside his new employer to a two storey brick building attached to the stables and inside, to his astonishment, were stacks of well seasoned timber, including a stack of beautifully carved oak panels.

'These are for the dining room Charlie, but I don't know if there's enough, that's why I asked you to measure the size of the room, in case we require any more.'

Charlie was obviously delighted with being entrusted to tackle a job of this magnitude, particularly as this would be his first assignment for the firm of Earnshaw & Cartwright. 'By, you must have thought a lot about old Sam's workmanship to give me a job such as this, considering you have never even seen any of my work yet,' he enthused.

William smiled knowingly, as he watched Charlie stroke the carved panels. 'Don't worry, when you told me Sam had left his house and workshop and his business to you, that was quite good enough for me. Now I suppose you will be needing a hand with a job this size?'

'Yes, I certainly will, but first I shall require a pony and trap, to fetch all my tools from town.'

'Right, you can have the trap, and I will arrange for a man and a lad to come off the estate on Monday afternoon, then you can keep them as long as you want. That's settled then. Now how about a ride?'

'Just a minute William,' said Charlie, as the older man moved towards the open door. 'I presume I shall be staying here until the dining room is finished. If that is the case, where am I going to sleep?'

'Why man, where you slept last night of course. What's the matter, don't you like the room?'

'Yes of course I like the room. As a matter of fact, I could easily become quite attached to it. It's perfect, too perfect for me, though ideal for a guest, not for a tradesman. You see, when I'm working, I don't wear clothes like these, you know, and I often work late. It would be impossible for me to wash and change every night, in time for dinner at eight.'

William stroked his chin meditatively. 'I see,' he said. 'Well, there's a nice tidy sized room above this place. Old Ned and his wife lived in it for years, but they both died some time ago and it has remained empty ever since.' Walking to the rear of the building, he said over his shoulder. 'Look here, I'll show you now,' and he began climbing some stairs which Charlie had somehow missed earlier. Reaching the top, he pushed up a wooden trap door and flung it wide open.

Charlie followed. He was pleasantly surprised

by the size of the room, and pleased to see it contained a double bed, wardrobe and washstand. There was even a fireplace with a small cooking range and, though the windows were dirty and cobwebbed, there was ample daylight coming through.

After a walk round and a few minutes inspection, Charlie turned to his employer. 'Yes William, this will suit me fine. Thank you very much.'

'Right, I think you had better fetch your things Monday morning Charlie, then spend the rest of that day making this place habitable. I will tell Lottie to send one of the maids over with some clean bedding for you.' Then, as an after thought. 'And I won't send anyone from the estate until Tuesday morning. I don't think you will be ready to start before then,' he chuckled, as he looked around him.

Charlie thought a moment, pondering over these remarks of William's. He realised, if he was to continue the search for the reason of his father's death, he needed to be in town, not marooned out here in the country, miles from anywhere.

'Would it be possible for me to take the trap and fetch my tools this morning? Then I can spend the weekend cleaning this place up, and be ready to start work on the dining room first thing Monday morning.'

William eyed him speculatively. He didn't have many men in his employ, who were so eager to commence work, and he certainly had no desire to stand in the way of such rare enthusiasm. 'Yes, that will suit me fine, Charlie. Come along and I will give you a hand to harness the pony.'

So Charlie drove into Hull, and collected his tools and a few clothes, and asked Lucy to keep his room for him. She was dreadfully upset because he was leaving, but brightened up considerably, when he assured her he would only be away for a short while.

He drove quickly on his return journey to Mount Pleasant, arriving just in time for the midday meal.

Charlie stayed one more night in the house, then moved his things out the next morning, and spent the rest of that day, cleaning out his new abode.

William sent along a man and a lad on the Monday morning as promised and by Thursday night they had completed approximately one third of the panelling.

Kate was so impressed by the speed and quality of Charlie's workmanship, she suggested to her father that he sail the *Elizabeth Kate* home on the Friday afternoon, and they all go for a sail up the River Humber at the weekend.

Charlie was very impressed by the size of the yacht and the easy way in which she handled, and he was looking forward to a further trip the next day.

The day dawned sunny and calm and, after Lottie, Kate and the children's nanny had carried hampers and baskets of food and drink on board, Charlie cast off and they moved slowly away from the bank.

Because the day was so calm, William had been up early to raise sufficient steam for the boiler. For, though the boat had twin masts, the sails would have been useless on a day such as this.

Jon and Beth were very excited, running around the deck laughing and shouting, and generally creating mayhem. In fact by the time the hillside of Watersmeet hove into view, their nanny was practically worn out, and was secretly wishing everyone had stayed at home.

William cut off the engine and gently brought her to rest by the jetty which jutted out into deep water, immediately below the village of Watersmeet. They could easily see the church and several houses built along the hill top, and could even hear the church clock as it struck twelve o'clock, in the still air.

After they had enjoyed their picnic sitting on the soft lush grass of the foreshore, William, Charlie and the children set off to climb the hill, leading to the village. On the way they saw many rabbits playing in the sand of their warrens, enjoying the warm sunshine, and the children shrieked with laughter as each one bolted down a hole, with just a flash of a white button of a tail, as they approached. The last part of the climb was quite steep, and the four of them were flushed and panting by the time they reached the top. The road, such as it was, joined the village street immediately behind the church.

They were walking past George Teanby's joiners workshop, thankful to be on level ground, when George looked up through his open workshop doorway, and saw them. 'Good day to you William Earnshaw,' he shouted.

William stopped, turned off the road and walked towards his friend, the children following, each of them holding one of Charlie's hands.

'Again I say, Good day to you William,' the man boomed. 'What the blazes are you doing wandering about here at this time on a Saturday afternoon? Have you no work to do, man?' he asked, shaking William warmly by the hand. He was a big, red-faced man with huge sideburns and a moustache, work worn apron and scarred bowler hat.

'Good day to you George Teanby. Yes I have plenty of work, thank you very much,' William laughingly replied. 'I would like you to meet Charlie Butlin, my new carpenter. He is panelling the dining room for us, you know with those oak panels I bought from you.'

A rare gleam of admiration shone in Charlie's eyes. 'So, you are the man who carved them panels? By, I wish I could carve oak like that,' he said, in a voice which showed great regard for the skill of a fellow craftsman.

'I see you still haven't done anything with that plot of land, you bought on the corner, William,' said George, angling for an order, for he was also a builder as well as a joiner and undertaker.

'No, I'm afraid I haven't had time yet, but don't worry George, when I decide what to do with it, you will be the first to know.'

After more small talk, during which Beth and Jon were becoming restless, William decided it was time to move on.

As Charlie pushed open the hill top gate, the children ran through and when they reached the edge of the hill, they began shouting and waving. 'I can see your ship, grandpa,' shouted Jon excitedly.

'I can see your ship too, grandpa,' parroted his sister, determined not to be ignored.

When William and Charlie joined the children, they stood in silent awe, stunned by the sheer beauty of the magnificent panorama laid out before them, for on a clear day it is still possible to see York Minster from that hill top! Then, lowering their gaze, they saw the *Elizabeth Kate*. She appeared so tiny and vulnerable anchored down there, by the bank of the sun-splashed waters of the Humber.

'God. What a picture!' said William softly. 'I would love a painting of this scene, just as it is today.'

At that moment they heard cries of delight behind them, and turning, watched as Jon and Beth set off to run round the Maze, or 'Julian's Bower,' as it is sometimes known. The two children called for the men to join them and, without hesitating they strolled over.

Charlie had never previously seen anything like this. 'Who cut this maze out of the turf in the first place, William?' he asked.

'Some local monks in the seventeenth century,' William replied.

Charlie was astounded. 'What!' he exclaimed. 'You mean to tell me that hundreds of kids, and possibly adults, have been running round this thing for all these years?'

'Yes Charlie, that is exactly what I'm telling you.'

They stood and watched as Beth and Jon carefully picked their way around the narrow twisting path, then simultaneously they both decided to look for the entrance and join them. Upon finding it, they followed the path, twisting and turning every which way, until finally, amid roars of laughter from Charlie and the two children, William became hopelessly lost right in the centre of the maze.

Unable to extricate himself, even with a modicum of dignity, and obviously having no idea which path to follow, he simply walked across the myriad of paths and climbed up the bank, accompanied by hoots of good natured derision from his two grandchildren and Charlie.

When the children had exhausted the novelty of this new and exciting game of finding their way out of the maze, William suggested they all walk along the well trodden hill top path. They had not gone very far however, before coming to the first 'Kissing Gate,' this being the first one Beth and Jon had ever seen. After William had explained the rules applying to such a gate, of course everyone had to have lots of hugs and kisses, interspersed with bouts of merriment and gales of laughter.

William couldn't forget that splendid view of the confluence of the three rivers from the hill top, and remembering what George Teanby had said about the plot of land he had bought on his last visit to Watersmeet, said, 'Come along now. I want to have a look at something in the village.'

Turning, they retraced their steps along the path and out through the gate, going a short way along the road until they came to a bend, it was here William stopped, for on this bend was the land he owned.

He stood on the opposite side of the road looking across at his land, and he visualised a tall three storey house standing there, with a window and a balcony in the room at the top, overlooking that wonderful panoramic view of the rivers, and the broad rolling acres of Yorkshire.

William became so engrossed in his thoughts and plans, he completely forgot about Charlie and the children, until Beth was standing beside him searching for his hand. 'Grandpa, I think it is time we were going. Mama will be getting very worried,' said the little girl, her upturned face flushed pink with the warm sun and the country air.

'Yes my dear, how very remiss of me. I'm afraid I became a little carried away with my plans, and never thought about the time,' said William, taking her hand and leading her down the road, and through the hill top gate once more, with Jon and Charlie following close behind.

Each of the men taking one of the children's hands, they proceeded diagonally across and down the steep hillside. By the time they arrived at the ship, they were all worn out and Charlie had to carry Beth for the last few hundred yards.

However, Lottie and Kate soon had a cup of tea and the inevitable buttered scones ready for them. Of course the children had far greater recuperative powers than their older escorts and, within minutes of arriving on board, they were chattering incessantly, excitedly telling Kate all about the afternoon's adventures. Especially that bit where grandpa got himself lost, right in the middle of the maze.

After the men had enjoyed a short rest, Lottie thought it was time to return home. So, while William started the engine, Charlie weighed anchor and, after turning the *Elizabeth Kate* around, they headed down river towards Hull.

Jon and Beth were fast asleep, lulled by the continuous throbbing of the engine when Mount Pleasant came into view, with the late afternoon sun glinting upon the glass in the dome and upstairs windows. They awoke however, when William guided his craft unerringly towards the jetty and, after a slight bump, Charlie leapt ashore to secure her mooring ropes.

As they were all waiting to step ashore, laden down with empty baskets and hampers, William asked if they had enjoyed the trip, and received such a chorus of affirmation, it was decided they would all have to do it again someday. And as he looked at the colour which had returned to his beloved daughter's cheeks, he knew the day had been well spent.

Charlie had told his employer about the girl he had met in Hull, and by the following Friday so much of the panelling had been completed, and he had worked so conscientiously and such long hours, William had decided to give him the weekend off. Borrowing one of the horses that Friday evening, Charlie rode to town and spent the weekend with Lucy.

She followed him upstairs to his room, and immediately the door closed, began to undress, for Lucy had no inhibitions with regard to her body. Charlie lay on the bed and feasted his eyes upon her in blatant admiration, then feeling his loins begin to stir, quickly followed suit.

She was like a demented feline, purring and scratching, as she drove her nails ever deeper into the flesh of his broad back.

Later, feeling sublimely happy and totally fulfilled, she lay beside him and gently stroked his heaving perspiring body. 'That was wonderful Charlie, thank you,' she murmured. 'You don't know how much I have missed you. I really do love you so much. It has been terrible having to sleep alone, and I have something to tell you.'

She was sitting up now, but Charlie pulled her down again and kissed her. At last she desisted, and sitting up once more, turned and looked down on him, her languorous eyes washing over him, and mirroring all the pent-up feeling of her love for him. Suddenly, for the first time in his long and chequered life, Charlie Butlin had the strangest sensation, and though he had never previously felt this way toward anyone, he recognised it immediately, and knew he was in love with this lovely girl.

As he lay there looking up at her, he realised he had been in love from the first day they met. Looking deep into his eyes, she smiled secretly to herself, as she saw the subtle change in his expression, and knew intuitively what had wrought this change.

Her heart sang as he gently took her hand and softly spoke her name, in a tone of voice she had never heard him use before. 'Lucy my love, did you say you had something to tell me?'

She gripped his hand as a tremor shook her frame. *'She had forgotten. God! How could she forget?'*

'What is it Lucy? Are you all right?' his concern for her evident in his change of tone.

'Yes, I . . . ' She bit her lip, hesitated, then plunged on. 'I . . . I'm going to have a baby. *Your* baby, Charlie!' Trembling now, she watched him keenly, waiting for the inevitable explosion which she was sure would ensue, following her revelation.

For a long moment nothing happened, and she was about to ask if he had heard what she said, when suddenly he erupted into peals of unrestrained laughter. Pulling her down, he made love to her again. It was even better than the last time, and when it was over, she looked at him, her eyes shining with happiness.

'Why, Mr Butlin, whatever was all that about?' she asked coyly.

'Just to make sure the other wasn't a false alarm,' he replied laughingly.

Lucy turned on her side and looked into his eyes, and now in a more serious vein, said quietly. 'It's true Charlie. I am pregnant, and a few months from now you will be the father of our baby,' she paused momentarily, then continued. 'What do you propose to do about this situation, Mr Charlie Butlin?'

He smiled, a long slow captivating kind of smile. 'Do?' he echoed. 'Why the same as every other respectable couple does, when faced with this problem. Get married of course!'

For a moment Lucy was almost overwhelmed. She could not believe he had spoken the words she had so longed to hear, then with tears in her eyes, she collapsed in his arms, her cup of happiness filled to the brim.

As a result of all the pent-up emotion which had built up within her, through the many sleepless nights, spent wondering what he would say when told of her condition, she began to tremble again.

However, the aftermath of this sudden release proved too much for her and she lay sobbing her heart out and, in between her sobs, whispering his name over and over again.

At last, showing uncharacteristic patience and great tenderness, he soothed her trembling naked body, then pulled the bed covers over her to keep her warm. Shortly afterwards, she drifted into a fitful sleep, with just a half smile touching her sensuous lips.

Charlie lay and watched her. He couldn't believe his luck as he lay there thinking about the forthcoming marriage. Since boyhood Charlie Butlin had always had an eye for the main chance and, though he had persuaded himself that he loved this girl, the fact she was the daughter and only child, of the owner and landlady of this inn, had not escaped his mercenary mind.

Eventually however, he too fell into an untroubled sleep, punctuated by pleasant dreams of himself as landlord of the Rose and Crown.

Fortunately for Lucy, upon Charlie's arrival that evening, her mother had given her the weekend off, and because of the previous emotional upheaval she had suffered, appertaining to her expected confrontation with Charlie, which of course had never transpired, she slept soundly that night, as though drugged.

Charlie, because of his strenuous efforts in the dining room at Mount Pleasant during the week, and then his more recent, even greater exertions in bed, also slept soundly without stirring, until suddenly the raucous booming of the gong downstairs, summoning the guests for breakfast, shattered their idyllic slumbers.

Leaping out of bed, they quickly washed and dressed and hurried down to the dining room for breakfast, Lucy going through to the kitchen to order some extra for her and Charlie, for they were both *raven*ously hungry.

Later that morning, Charlie took her to a jewellers and bought her an engagement ring. Lucy gasped at the price he paid, for she had no idea of the thousands he had tucked away in the bank. She only wore one glove all the way home, for she could not resist continually glancing at those sparkling diamonds, set in that beautiful ring.

During their walk back to the inn, her feelings and emotions were strangely mixed. At one moment feeling excited and exhilarated, and the next serious and solemn, yet content and happy, secure in the knowledge that of all the men she had known, only Charlie had asked her to be his wife.

Lucy began to sing softly to herself. 'I'm having Charlie's baby. I'm having Charlie's baby, and nobody knows, and nobody knows.'

Charlie stopped and looked at her. 'What are you singing?' he asked. She sang the words again, louder this time. 'Keep that up and the whole damn town will know,' he chortled.

Suddenly she skipped away from him and, turning, began to walk backwards. 'Do you love me Charlie Butlin?' she asked precociously.

'Yes, you know I do. Now come here.'

'If you love me, prove it. Come here and kiss me,' she said, laughingly teasing him.

He caught her arm, and crushed her to him, kissing her long and passionately, right there in the middle of that busy street, watched by scores of staid horrified Victorians, on their way to and from the shops.

Charlie returned to Mount Pleasant on the Monday morning, and by Thursday afternoon had completed his work in the dining room. William and Lottie were so pleased with the overall effect of the panelling, they gave him five extra sovereigns for doing such a fine job.

As Charlie was packing away his tools, William came and asked his advice on how to remove an old tree stump, from near the side of the house. He took him to see the offending bole. It was massive.

'Only one way to do this job,' said Charlie laconically. 'Dynamite!'

'Dynamite!' echoed William incredulously. 'Will that be safe?'

'Of course, if it is used correctly.'

'Could you do the job, Charlie? Have you used dynamite before?'

'Yes, many times when I was prospecting. Certainly I can do the job. Have you any dynamite here?'

'No, but there is plenty up at the quarry. Go saddle a horse, while I write you a note to take to the manager.'

Charlie returned an hour later with the dynamite, going straight up to his room to fetch some tools. Digging right beneath the stump, he placed a stick of dynamite under two sides of it. Laying only a short fuse, he lit it and ran.

The result was spectacular, for tree roots and debris came raining down on all sides, and where there had been a stubborn old tree stump, was now just a large hole.

William came dashing out, shouting and swearing. 'What the hell happened? You nearly frightened us all to death, man.' Then he saw the hole where the stump had been, and stopped short. 'By hell! that shifted it. Sorry I shouted at you Charlie, but I didn't know you had returned. You can go now if you wish. Take the trap to carry your tools, and thank you for solving this problem so expeditiously for me.' Then looking around him. 'I will instruct someone to clear all this up tomorrow.'

As Charlie was walking away, his employer called after him. 'Thank you once again for the dining room Charlie, you really have done a very good job. Oh, and Charlie, don't bother to come in tomorrow. In fact, take the rest of this week off, you have certainly earned it.'

Charlie thanked him and went to hitch up the trap. He was lifting in his tool kit, when a big chestnut horse came cantering into the courtyard. He knew good horse flesh when he saw it, and he stood in silent admiration as he watched the rider bring him to a halt.

His admiration heightened as the man athletically dismounted and Charlie saw the size of him, for his height and breadth of shoulders, almost matched those of his horse.

At that moment Charlie's unspoken question was answered, for the head groom hurried from his tack room. Through long experience Fred Allsop had learned to recognise the hoofbeats of his master's horse, and touching his cap, he moved swiftly to the horse's head and addressing the stranger, said. 'It's good to see you. Welcome home, Master Thomas.'

Just then, Kate and the two children rushed out of the house. 'Papa, Papa,' they shouted excitedly, but Kate was the first to reach him. Thomas picked her up as easily as he would a child, held her close and kissed her. Then he did the same with Beth and Jon.

Charlie stepped up into the trap and drove out of the courtyard, away from that happy domestic scene. Going down the drive, he mused aloud. 'So, that's the great Thomas Cartwright. By hell, I wouldn't like to tangle with him.' The disturbed rooks, high in the tree tops above him, answered mockingly with their incessant *Caw Caw, Caw Caw*, and though the evening was warm, for no reason he could comprehend, Charlie Butlin shivered as he listened to their abrasive cry. Whipping the pony into a fast trot, eager to get away from the gloom of those overhanging trees, Charlie only relaxed when he reached the open road.

When he arrived at the inn, Charlie was confronted by desperate scenes of tears and despair. Lucy, tear stained and hollow eyed, fell into his arms almost before he managed to get through the door, and began to babble incoherently about her mother.

He dispatched a servant to bring in his tools and trunk, and then return the pony and trap to Earnshaw & Cartwright's shipyard. Then, supporting Lucy, he practically carried her to his room, and after forcing her to drink a stiff brandy, he at last began to make some sense out of her wailing.

Her mother had not been feeling well that morning and had returned to her bedroom for a rest. However, when Lucy had called in to see how she was sometime later, apparently she had died in her sleep. The doctor had been summoned, and had concluded her death was due to a heart attack. She had never been a strong woman and, after the death of her husband, had struggled to continue running the inn on her own, until Lucy was old enough to help. But the daily grind of those earlier years had taken its toll, and though the spirit had been willing, in the end the work had proved too much.

When Charlie had finally assimilated all the facts, he immediately took charge of the inn, and of the funeral arrangements. He sent a servant to the doctors for a sedative to help Lucy sleep, and then helped to serve behind the bar for the rest of that night.

On the Monday morning Charlie went to the yard to see William and, after explaining his current domestic situation, his employer graciously gave him the week off.

One month after the funeral of her mother, Charlie and Lucy were married, but for reasons known only to himself, he insisted she keep her own name and be known as Mrs Myers.

On that Monday morning before Charlie had arrived, William had completed several sketches of the house he wished to build on his plot of land at Watersmeet. He had then taken them through to his draughtsmen in the drawing office, and explained his requirements, telling them the plans must be finished by last thing Wednesday night.

After informing Lottie he would be away on business for one night, William left early on the Thursday morning and caught the ferry to New Holland. From there he went by train to Barton-on-Humber, where he hired a good horse to take him to Watersmeet.

George Teanby was rather surprised, though pleased to see him. Especially when he presented him with one hundred sovereigns, along with the new plans. William quickly told his friend the money was not just as a deposit, but also to help expedite the building of his house.

'I can assure you William, the money will help, but looking at these plans, I'm going to need a bit more than this. How the devil

73

do you expect me to build a house this high?' asked George as he scrutinised the plans.

William smiled. 'Why, that shouldn't be a problem for you George. You're always telling me your village church was built in the eleventh century, so if them old codgers could do it then, I'm sure you can today.'

Mrs Teanby came out of the house to inform them lunch was ready, and her husband being in an expansive mood, because of the order he had just received, invited William to stay.

The two friends spent the rest of that day marking out the foundations of the proposed house, on William's plot. They marked out the garden and the paths, William even had a prepared list of all the flowers and shrubs he required planting. It soon became obvious to George, that his new client had no intention of returning home that night. So, William stayed the night with them, and they thoroughly enjoyed talking over old times well into the early hours.

After breakfast the following morning, William was on the point of leaving when a sudden thought struck him. Backing his horse up to the workshop doors, where George was putting new spokes in a wagon wheel, he leaned down from the saddle. 'Just one small item old friend. On no account, send any mail appertaining to this contract to my home. Send everything direct to my office at the shipyard. You see, this house is a present for Lottie, and I want it to be a complete surprise.'

In early spring the following year, Lucy gave birth to a beautiful baby girl, and Charlie absolutely adored her. For though he would not allow his wife to use his name, he really worshipped her and could not do enough for Lucy and the child.

Some weeks later, when Lucy had regained her strength and svelte figure, she and Charlie took their baby to church and had her christened Ruth Charlotte Myers.

Charlie Butlin's life was running very smoothly now, for with his money he had given the old inn a new front, installed good reliable bar staff, a splendid new cook and a trustworthy caring nanny to help Lucy with the baby. He had a good relationship with his employers, and was liked and respected by the men, the only blot upon his horizon being the fact that he was no nearer discovering the cause of his father's death, or even the location of his grave until Ruth was one year old.

On that particular evening, Charlie was sitting alone in the bar having a quiet drink, when an old man walked in and stood looking around, as though searching for someone.

Eventually, his tired old eyes settled upon Charlie, and he shuffled over. 'Are you the young fella that's been asking about the death of your father?' he croaked, his voice easily matching his years.

Charlie sat bolt upright, his gaze riveted on the old man's wrinkled features. 'Yes I am,' he replied. 'Why, do you know something?' he asked sharply.

The old man sat down, and a smile creased his weather-beaten face, showing his two remaining front teeth, which reminded Charlie of a couple of rotting fence posts. 'Not so fast my lad,' the man croaked, his voice strangely faint. He tapped his throat. 'It's me tonsils. They need lubricating like. Just fetch me a mug of ale and a glass of whisky. Then I'll tell you everything you want to know,' he whispered.

An hour later, after the old man had left, suitably imbibed with alcohol, Charlie sat on alone with his thoughts. His first reaction to the story of his father's death, had been vicious anger and an all consuming feeling for instant revenge.

After a while however, he calmed down, and began to evolve a scheme so fraught with death and destruction in its concept, and yet if he could succeed, so brilliant in its execution, no one would ever suspect his involvement.

His heart was now full of an overpowering black hatred, for all those responsible in the matter of his father's death and the subsequent removal of the body. Though outwardly he remained calm, and carried out his duties at work in his usual efficient manner, he was quite content to bide his time and wait for that vital moment, when he could put his devastating plan into operation and, though Charlie lived only for that time, neither his work rate or his marriage were affected.

He had no thought of compassion for those who were destined to survive his horrific revenge scheme, for their lifelong misery and suffering was the pivotal point of the whole plan. Sometimes at night, when Lucy was asleep, he would literally hug himself with glee, at the prospect of watching the perpetrators of his father's foul murder, slowly pine away and die of loneliness and grief.

Charlie had to wait another fifteen months before he could put his heinous plan into operation and, though during that time he had a golden opportunity to wreak his revenge upon at least one of the culprits, he stayed his hand.

For he remembered an old maxim Sam had drilled into him. 'If you ever make a plan to do something, Charlie,' he had said, 'and after examining it from all possible angles, you decide it is a good plan, no matter who or what comes along to side-track you, always remember your original plan and stick to it.'

So Charlie Butlin waited, the fire of his hatred never being dimmed by time, but on the contrary, burning ever more fiercely because of the waiting.

2

Some ten years had elapsed since Kate and Thomas had returned from their honeymoon. Years which had seen great changes at Mount Pleasant. For, during their first two years of marriage, Elizabeth and then Jon had been born, bringing the old house to life with the noise of chattering, screaming children.

Immediately Kate was well enough to travel after her second confinement, she visited Maria, to ask her advice on how not to have a new baby every year, which seemed to be the normal way of married life for the majority of her contemporaries.

Now, though Maria had appeared to be helpful in every respect with her advice, in reality she was being rather coy and more than a little unscrupulous, when she suggested Kate should allow her husband to make love to her on only two particular occasions of each month, knowing full well that Thomas would never agree to such treatment, and that eventually he would seek to assuage his phenomenal sexual appetite elsewhere.

Of course that is precisely what happened. Consequently, Kate had no more children, and Maria's love life was once again complete.

Meanwhile, William had completed Lottie's surprise house at Watersmeet and, though he raved on enthusiastically about the wonderful panoramic view from the top floor window, Lottie would have none of it, and absolutely refused to go anywhere near the place. Though William pleaded, cajoled and threatened, she resolutely refused to give any rational explanation for her total abhorrence of the village, much to the chagrin of William, and this had resulted in a family rift, which had dogged the otherwise domestic bliss for many months.

Finally, in late autumn, following the completion of the much maligned High House, Lottie had an inspiration, and this had culminated in William being invited into the library on that particular Christmas morning to receive his present.

He stood transfixed, his features a caricature of dismayed incredulity, as he gazed up at the large oil painting hanging above the fireplace. It was a painting of his favourite view from the hill top at Watersmeet, complete with the *Elizabeth Kate* moored by the foreshore of the River Humber, drawing the viewer's eye down the hill right to the centre of the picture, and the setting sun seeming to beautify the whole panorama with a crimson magnificence, turning the Humber into a river of molten lava.

William just stood and stared. The picture was breathtaking in its portrayal of the scene he had witnessed that day when he, Charlie and the children had climbed the hill to Watersmeet.

No! He was wrong. That couldn't be, for that had been around noon. Then he recollected. How he had expounded to Lottie about it on the way home, and what a perfect picture it would make in the setting sun. And she had remembered!

From that day forth, sanity and love had returned to Mount Pleasant, and the house at Watersmeet had become nothing more than a bad memory, though occasionally, but never in the presence of William, it had been referred to as 'William's Folly.'

As the family stood grouped around the roaring log fire on that Christmas morning, enthralled by the new painting, not one of them could possibly have visualised the years of heartbreak, one of their members was destined to suffer, sitting at the top floor window, gazing forlornly down upon this very same view.

Lottie had turned one of the spare bedrooms into a schoolroom, and for several years she had taught Elizabeth and Jon, the rudiments of English, French and Maths. However, Elizabeth would be twelve years old in March, and next September she would be leaving home to attend a private boarding school for young ladies. This was a prospect which filled Lottie with sadness, for she had grown very fond of this lovely girl, with her fair looks, and such a pleasant, trusting, sunny nature.

There was only thirteen months' difference in the ages of the two children, so Jon would be eleven in April and, as he had shown more than a passing interest in the building of ships, Thomas had decided to enrol him at Trinity House, hoping he would eventually follow in his father's footsteps.

Thomas had never really taken to Charlie Butlin, the man his partner had employed while he and Bull were away on one of their numerous voyages to Europe. Even though William often took Charlie deep sea fishing at weekends in the *Elizabeth Kate*, and the two men were obviously firm friends, somehow Thomas could never bring himself to completely trust Charlie, and he found it very difficult to give a reasonable explanation for his gut feeling of mistrust.

However, the feeling persisted, for he could not seem to forgive the way this usurper had ingratiated himself into the lives and minds of all the family at Mount Pleasant with his outrageous tales of his life and exploits in Australia.

Much to the annoyance of Thomas, Kate always spoke very highly of her 'friend Charlie,' and even the children called him Uncle Charlie. However, Thomas had to abruptly change his attitude, and his feeling of animosity toward Charlie, one very cold frosty morning in early March.

Thomas, Walt the yard foreman, and Charlie were walking along the dock, watching a trawler coming in for some minor repairs, when suddenly Walt slipped on a patch of ice, and as he was falling over the edge, he made a grab at the arm of Thomas, causing them both to crash down to the icy waters below.

By this time, the ship was only a couple of yards from the dockside, and drifting inexorably towards the trapped men.

Showing remarkable presence of mind, and instant reaction, Charlie snatched two empty barrels, which fortunately had been left standing on the dock, and hurled them over the side, at the same time shouting desperately for a rope.

Thomas and Walt each managed to turn the barrels so their ends were pressing against the dock wall, thus preventing themselves being crushed between the ship's side and the wall.

At that moment, Bull arrived with a rope, and he and Charlie hauled up the two dripping men and, as they were pulling Thomas over the edge, the barrels below shattered and splintered into a hundred pieces under the terrific pressure, the ship almost trapping the legs of Thomas as they pulled him clear. They were both blue with cold, and were quickly rushed to William's office, where fortunately a good fire was blazing in the grate.

After stripping off their wet clothes, they were each given a large towel which William had miraculously produced from somewhere. Then they spent the rest of that morning wrapped in a towel, whilst waiting for their clothes to dry.

Thomas felt rather guilty about the way he had behaved towards Charlie Butlin in the past and, later that afternoon when he was alone, he sent for him to come to the office. Moments later there was a knock on the door, and before he could answer, Charlie walked in.

Thomas was standing with his back to

the fire apparently none the worse for his traumatic experience of the morning. He stepped forward and held out his hand. 'Thank you, Charlie,' he greeted him warmly. 'You probably saved our lives today, and if not, certainly a few crushed ribs anyway.'

Charlie was clearly embarrassed. 'Oh, I don't know. I only did what anyone else would have done. I just happened to be in the right place at the right time, that's all, Thomas.'

'Yes, that's as may be, but there aren't many men working here, who would have reacted as quickly or as efficiently as you did. Anyway, I thank you on behalf of Walt and myself.'

Charlie made no reply, so Thomas continued. 'I'm sorry Charlie if I haven't been over friendly towards you in the past, but I promise you that will all change from this day forward.'

'Don't worry about it Thomas, I was a boss once and it never pays to get too friendly with the workers, though I must admit, things were very different down under.'

'What do you mean different? How were they different, Charlie?'

Charlie hesitated, but only for a second. 'Well you see, Thomas,' he began. 'It's like this. Now that's the first thing. You don't really like me calling you Thomas. You would prefer me to call you Master Thomas like everyone else does around here, but in Australia people aren't like that. You see it is a new country, populated by comparatively young new people, all starting as equals, right from the bottom, and there are no toffee nosed aristocrats telling them what to do. In short, there is no 'Them and Us' syndrome.'

Thomas smiled at the man's frankness. 'You wouldn't call me a toffee nosed aristocrat, would you Charlie?' he asked softly.

Charlie looked up at this powerfully built giant of a man, standing so nonchalantly before him. He had encountered men such as this in the gold fields, who were the most dangerous when they were calm and spoke softly, but never, he reflected grimly, of the stature and obvious strength of Thomas Cartwright.

He involuntarily took a step backwards, and averted his eyes from those twin shafts of blue steel, which seemed to bore into his soul. 'No, of course not,' he stammered. 'I was just trying to make a point. Or possibly an excuse for being too familiar,' he added lamely.

Thomas laughed. The tension was broken,

and Charlie thankfully relaxed. 'All right Charlie, you have made your point, and I understand, but you have to realise we must insist on discipline in a yard as large as this, otherwise we should have complete chaos, for as you well know, familiarity breeds contempt.'

As Charlie walked through the outer office and down the steps, he tried to imagine anyone in his right mind being contemptible of the man he had just left, though as he reached the bottom step, he allowed himself a smug satisfied smile. For fate had been kind to him that day, enabling him to bridge the gap of mistrust, which he had always felt existed between himself and Thomas Cartwright.

The following week, the son of Bull, and young Miles, were sailing with their fathers to Europe. They were both well into their teens by now, and having completed several years study at Trinity House, were quite ready for some practical seagoing experience.

Having grown up together at Maria's cottage, the two were great friends and almost inseparable. They were both big lads for their age, each one resembling his father in looks and build, and they had been looking forward to this voyage with mounting excitement for some weeks.

There had been some emotional moments at the cottage on the evening prior to their departure, between Maria, Annie and the two boys, and none of them managed much sleep that night. However, next morning they were up early, as fresh as usual, and could hardly wait for Annie to come out and drive them to town in the trap.

Thomas had asked Maria to stay at home because no one at the yard knew of his relationship with Miles, but several were aware of his association with Maria, and wanting to keep Miles' true identity a secret, he had no wish for the boy to be seen with his mother, not in the vicinity of the shipyard anyway.

The lads were young and strong, and they both thoroughly enjoyed the voyage, proving very useful in the running of the ship, and learning more about the sea, the wind and the stars with each day and night that passed. So much so in fact that Thomas and Bull, who were pleased and very proud of the way they had handled themselves, decided to take them on all future voyages.

3

During a hot dry spell in the middle of July the following year, William had sent Thomas and Bull to the Horse Fair at Howden, for the purpose of buying three horses, two for himself and one for a farmer friend who lived near the River Trent at Burton-on-Stather.

Meanwhile, on the Friday morning of that week, William had suggested that he and Charlie should take the family for a trip up the Humber in the *Elizabeth Kate* on Saturday, providing the weather held good.

There was no apparent reason to suppose the weather would change, so they finished work early that afternoon, and sailed the yacht home to her moorings situated just below Mount Pleasant.

The following morning dawned bright and clear, with no sign of a breeze, so Charlie hurried down to the *Elizabeth Kate*, to get the boiler going, for it was obvious they would have to use the engine.

At last they were all on board, and Charlie was just about to cast off when, amidst much shouting telling him to wait, a red-faced, agitated youth skidded to a halt, on a heaving, lathered horse.

'Where's Mr Earnshaw?' he panted excitedly, as he leapt to the ground.

'I'm here,' said William, appearing on deck, and recognising the youth as an apprentice from the yard. 'What is it, lad?'

'Fire, sir!' came the startling reply. 'That Russian ship moored in the dock, she's ablaze in the forrard hold!'

William didn't hesitate. He scrambled on to the jetty, then turned to Charlie. 'You take the ship Charlie, and take this lad with you. I shall have to go to the yard.'

Lottie and Kate protested, and reminded him he had been looking forward to this day's outing, just as much as they, but William was adamant.

'Sorry, but I shall have to go. I am still the boss, and in an emergency such as this, my place is with the men. Charlie will look after you. He is quite capable, and give this lad a drink Kate. He looks all in,' and after that last remark he leapt upon the youth's horse, and whipped him into a fast gallop towards Hull.

Charlie made some excuse about having left something in his old room above the stables, and hurried away towards the house, returning a few moments later carrying a mysterious brown paper parcel, which he immediately took below and stowed away in a cabin, locking the door on his way out.

Coming up on deck, he ordered the lad to cast off, and with loud cheers from the children, the ship slowly pulled away from the jetty.

By noon of that day, Thomas and Bull had crossed the River Trent via the ferry to Burton Stather and, after delivering their purchase to William's farmer friend, sat and enjoyed a well earned mug of ale and a sandwich outside the Ferryboat Inn.

After the horses had been fed, watered and rested, and the 'inner man' satisfied, at least temporarily, the two friends were mounted and on their way, climbing the hill diagonally towards the path running along the top, straight to Watersmeet.

They were walking along in single file because of the narrow path, and were just passing Kell Well, a favourite haunt of generations of children and adults searching for 'Stars' and 'Fossils' in the bed of the running stream which, as legend says, 'has never been known to run dry,' when a muffled explosion startled all four horses.

'What the hell was that?' shouted Bull, struggling desperately to control his mount.

'I don't know. It seemed to come from somewhere ahead and below us. There, look there is smoke coming from near the Humber.'

Bull's gaze followed the pointing finger of his friend, and saw a huge pall of black smoke rising up into the warm afternoon air.

The two friends urged their horses forward at a fast gallop, oblivious of the lower tree branches lashing them in the face, or the thorn bushes piercing their riding breeches. Quite unexpectedly, they emerged from the trees and thick undergrowth, and looking down the hill could see the cause of the smoke, for there appeared to be a ship on fire moored by the river bank, and she was blazing from stem to stern.

Suddenly, a light, offshore breeze caused a break in the smoke, enabling them to see twin masts, and the outline of the doomed ship's hull.

'My God! That's the *Elizabeth Kate!*' screamed Thomas. His words were almost lost to Bull, for Thomas had cut the loose horse free, and was tearing down the steep hillside towards the burning ship, giving no regard for his own safety or that of his plunging mount.

Miraculously they both reached the bottom safely, and went full gallop across the level terrain, and then along the foreshore. As he arrived at the stricken vessel, he reined in his horse to a slithering shuddering halt, leaping off and running forward.

Thomas could see immediately that if anyone had been on board, nothing could be done to save them now, for the ship was a blazing blackened hulk, with all her superstructure and half the deck torn away by the force of the explosion.

A voice behind him said quietly. 'Thomas,' and he turned to see Bull pointing at two still, small figures lying on their backs in the soft green grass of the foreshore.

Thomas rushed over. They were his children, Elizabeth and Jon, and they appeared to be sleeping but, as he bent lower he felt a knife thrust deep in his heart, for they were not sleeping and, though completely unmarked, they were both dead!

A terrible cry of anguish rent the air, and long agonising sobs racked his huge frame, as he lifted the bodies of his two beloved children and gently cradled them in his arms.

Bull could only stand helplessly by and watch the traumatic suffering of his friend, for he knew no words of sympathy which would be of any comfort or consolation to Thomas at this terrible moment.

A small group of people from the village,

who had heard the explosion and then, seeing the subsequent fire, had rushed down the hillside to see if they could help. Now they were all huddled together as though for protection from the grief of this apparently demented giant of a man who seemed to be the dead children's father.

At that moment someone arrived with a horse and cart from Flats Farm, and Bull, with great difficulty, managed to persuade Thomas to lay the bodies of his two children on some clean straw, which someone had thoughtfully placed in the bottom of the cart.

As Thomas turned away, he saw something sticking out of the mud and, recognising it as one of Kate's boots, flung himself down on the grass and found he could just manage to reach it. The sole of the boot was uppermost and as Thomas pulled, it emitted a horrible sucking sound, as though the mud was loath to give up its macabre prize.

At last, the boot was clear, and as Thomas dragged it towards him he uttered a terrifying, almost inhuman scream, as his bulging eyes locked onto the boot's ghastly contents.

Bull dropped to his knees beside his friend, and his face paled beneath its tan as he stared in horror at the thing Thomas was holding. *For Kate's foot and part of her leg were still inside the tightly laced up boot. Her leg had been torn off just below the knee by the explosion!*

Thomas staggered to his feet, his hands and shirt splattered with mud and his dead wife's blood, and the villagers huddled closer together with fear, as this Colossus drew himself to his full height and throwing back his head, cursed the God in heaven for allowing this tragedy to happen, at the same time beating his massive chest with the grisly object he held in his hand.

Bull stood and watched, numb with shock and not knowing what to do to help his friend in this, his greatest hour of need.

One of the group of onlookers suddenly sneezed and Thomas, apparently realising for the first time that he and Bull were not alone, and showing a remarkable sense of willpower, and consummate strength of character, abruptly ceased his volatile vilification of his God and, lowering his leonine head, allowed his glazed eyes to flicker over the small knot of villagers.

After a moment, pregnant with silent, almost tactile emotion, except for the hissing and burning of the stricken ship, he stiffened as his gaze came to rest upon the abject figure of a man cowering on his knees, in the middle of the group.

All the hostility he had felt towards this man in the past, and the fact that he had never really trusted him, suddenly boiled over as he thought he had found the person responsible for all his suffering and the terrible loss of all those he had loved.

'*Charlie Butlin! Come here!*' The words were spat out with such venom and resonance of authority, that the group involuntarily stepped back, leaving Charlie vulnerable and isolated.

Thomas stood and waited, his eyes clear now, his only thought to wreak vengeance upon this craven, miserable creature before him. Charlie began to move and, very slowly, he actually crawled towards his employer dragging an empty can, all the while mouthing incoherent sentences.

When he came within reach, Thomas bent down and, grabbing him by the collar, roughly hauled the man to his feet. 'What the hell are you doing here, Butlin?' he rasped.

Charlie made an effort to reply, but couldn't seem to form the words and, as Thomas released his hold, would have fallen if Bull hadn't leapt forward and caught him.

Thomas slapped him sharply on the cheek with the palm of his hand. 'Come along man, speak. Why the devil are you carrying that empty can?'

Charlie appeared to be in deep shock. However, the mention of the can seemed to trigger some latent mental process, and he looked down at the can as though aware of it for the first time. His features cleared as his eyes lost their blank look and resumed their normal crafty, slightly malevolent expression.

He pushed Bull aside, and now able to stand on his own, he flung the empty can into the river, and though obviously still in some kind of shock began to speak, but in sharp short staccato like sentences.

'This morning. We go sailing. We stop here for drinking water, for Mrs Earnshaw.'

Thomas grabbed the wretch and shook him. 'Mrs Earnshaw!' he echoed. 'Do you mean my Aunt Lottie was on board the *Elizabeth Kate*?'

Charlie nodded dumbly, and Thomas drew back his arm, with the intention of splattering a fair amount of Charlie Butlin over a large tract of the foreshore.

Bull, however, moved quickly forward to intervene. 'Wait a minute Thomas,' he said sharply. 'This cretin will be no use to us, if you knock him out.'

Thomas obediently allowed his arm to fall. He was now beginning to feel the strain of the last half hour, and willingly left the questioning to his friend.

Bull spun the man round and faced him. 'Was William on board?' he asked bluntly.

Charlie stared at him, then continued speaking in the same peculiar manner. 'No. He called to yard. We going on board. Man rode up. Said ship on fire in dock. So William not come.'

At that moment, Thomas noticed the horse and cart in which he had earlier placed the bodies of his two children.

'Charlie. Why did you go all the way up to the village for water, when there is a farm just a short distance along the foreshore?'

The voice was soft and sibilant, almost caressing in its intonation, and Charlie immediately recognised the danger signals. He was not a small man by any means, and could hold his own against most men, but he was sensible enough to realise he would have no chance in a fight with either of these two.

With his cunning brain working overtime, he decided to prevaricate, and somehow to lie his way out of this seemingly impossible, yet deadly situation. 'Me wanted to, sir,' he whined, pretending to humble himself. 'But Mrs Earnshaw, she say no. Water must come from village.'

Bull could see they were getting nowhere questioning Charlie Butlin, and suggested they all leave and climb the hill up to Watersmeet. Meanwhile, the two loose horses he and Thomas had bought in Howden, had caught up and were now munching the grass nearby. However he easily managed to catch hold of each halter, and tie them to the back of the cart.

It was a strange bizarre scene, as the sad little procession wound its weary way ever upward towards the village, with the still smouldering, smoking shell of the once elegantly beautiful *Elizabeth Kate* forming a sombre backcloth.

When they reached the village, a large, ruddy-faced man stepped forward. 'Ah, it's good to see you Charlie. I wondered what was happening when I saw you running out of the churchyard, looking all agitated and swinging an empty can. By the way, was William on board?'

Charlie's blood froze, but worse was to come, for before he could think of a suitable reply, a woman in the crowd which had gathered to await their arrival said. 'Yes Mr Teanby. I saw him an'all, running up the street he was like a bat out of hell, and as he reached the hill top the ship blew up, and he just hung on the gate screaming, 'No! No!' '

Charlie glanced furtively at Thomas and Bull, but apparently they were both so stricken with grief they seemed completely oblivious to everything around them. So, trying desperately to produce something approaching his normal voice, he said. 'Hello George. No William was not on board, he was called away at the last minute.'

George Teanby walked slowly over to the now stationary cart, for it had stopped to give the horses a breather. He paled perceptibly as he looked in, and recognised the two bodies.

'Was there anyone else, Charlie?' he asked, in a subdued voice as he turned away.

Charlie came closer. 'William's wife Lottie, and Kate, the wife of Thomas Cartwright,' he replied softly.

George stepped back, and leaned against the cart for support. 'My God! Not Lottie, and Kate! Are you sure, man?'

'Absolutely. There is no doubt about it, they have all gone.'

'What a terrible tragedy,' muttered the carpenter, wringing his work-callused hands. 'This news will finish William. His wife, his daughter and his grandchildren, all gone in one afternoon.'

He removed his hat, bowed his head and stood a moment as if in silent prayer, and then, having replaced his hat, walked over to Thomas.

He was stunned by the sight of his friend, for his face was tear stained and dirty. His shirt was soiled with dried mud and blood, and he appeared to have aged ten years in one afternoon. Though George was used to dealing with death, it was usually due to natural causes, and never on such a scale as this. Also these people were personal friends, for he and his wife had attended the weddings of both Lottie and Kate.

Assuming the guise of the caring, anxious undertaker, George Teanby gently placed a hand upon the arm of Thomas. He was well aware through long experience of dealing with the bereaved that any words of sympathy he may utter would evoke very little reaction, and in all probability only make matters much worse.

Thomas nodded in mute recognition as George removed his hand. 'I will attend to the children, Thomas,' he said kindly. 'But first I must send a rider on a fast horse to inform William of this terrible tragedy, then I will fetch a spare key he left with me, and take you and your men up to the new house.'

The house had been fully furnished throughout in readiness for Lottie's first visit, but of course she never came, and so it had remained, closed and silent, until now.

Even during the hot dry weather of high summer, the place seemed damp, cold and uninviting, so Bull, happy to find something to do, set about bringing in sticks and coal, and very soon had a good fire going in the kitchen range, and a similar one in the front room. While Charlie just sat and stared out of the window, speaking to no one, apparently in as great a state of shock as Thomas, and Bull could only assume he must be blaming himself for what had happened to the *Elizabeth Kate*.

In the meantime, Thomas couldn't seem to settle. He needed something to occupy his mind. Anything to help take it off that horrifying moment when he first saw the inside of poor Kate's boot. He suddenly had an irresistible urge to climb the stairs and look out from that top floor window at the view William had so often extolled to him.

There was a telescope lying on the table, and snatching it up, he crossed swiftly to the window. Adjusting the glass, he was amazed at the distance he could see from his lofty perch, and as he scanned the foreshore, he finally focused on a faint plume of smoke still rising from the smouldering tomb of his beloved Kate.

With a heart rending sob, Thomas hurled the telescope from him and sank wearily into a large comfortable leather chair, which someone had placed in a propitious position immediately facing the window.

The evening sun was sinking in the West, creating a false aura of peace and tranquility in the darkened room, when a hand was gently laid upon his shoulder, and a woman's voice softly murmured. 'Thomas, Thomas. Please wake up.'

As though in a dream, he stirred and cried out. *'Kate. Oh Kate! Thank God you have come!'*

He turned, his eyes and mind still cobwebbed with sleep, and gradually the full realisation of the horror which had so devastated his family earlier that day, dawned upon him, and at last he knew it could not be Kate standing there.

'Hello Maria,' he said in a strange, calm voice, almost as though he was a puppet, and the voice was being thrown by some unseen ventriloquist. 'I never expected to see you. How did you get here?' he continued in the same flat monotone.

Maria tasted the salt from her tear drenched cheeks and lips, for she had been crying most of the way here, ever since William had brought news of the terrible tragedy, and had called at the cottage to collect her and Annie, hoping they may help to keep himself and Thomas sane, and perhaps give a little moral support.

She tried desperately to control her emotions, and fight back the flood of tears which once again threatened to engulf her. 'William called at the cottage to bring the dreadful news, and asked Annie and I to accompany him. He thought that somehow we might be able to help.'

Maria was amazed at the calm way in which she had replied, for she felt sick and numb with grief at the suffering this man whom she loved more than life itself was enduring and, though she heard her words, she had great difficulty in believing it was she who had uttered them.

Thinking this was no time for platitudes or inane conversation, Maria decided to do something practical and, as she looked at the lamp standing on the table, she remembered seeing a metal holder containing matches. She removed the glass chimney and applied a lighted match to the wick, quickly turning it down to prevent the high flame blackening the glass, as she replaced it.

Maria sucked in her breath in disbelief as the lamplight flooded the room and she saw for the first time, the unkempt haggard appearance of her lover. 'Just stay there, please dearest. I won't be long,' she said softly, as she left the room.

Several minutes later, Maria returned carrying a jug of hot water, soap and a towel, and a change of clothes which, showing great foresight even in the hurry and fluster of leaving the cottage, she and Annie had thoughtfully remembered to pack.

Thomas sat silent and uncomplaining, as Maria removed his shirt and commenced to wash him. Her heart ached for him, as with her soft lathered hands she caressed those familiar rippling muscles, before giving him a good rub down with the large towel. He made no remonstrance when she unfastened his belt, and removed his boots and riding breeches.

'I think you can dress yourself now, Thomas,' she said huskily, handing him a clean shirt and trousers, for she was perspiring freely after her exertions, coupled with her climb up those two flights of stairs, and the close proximity of his naked body within the confines of this small room.

As he finished dressing, he turned to her, and in a hoarse whisper, spoke her name.

'*Maria!*' Instinctively, she went to him, and became enveloped in his all powerful embrace. But this was not the kind of passionate embrace between two lovers, which she had experienced so often in the past. No, this was different, very different. He was like a lost soul, silently crying out in despair for her companionship, pleading with her to share his grief and, though he had spoken no more than her name, she understood and reciprocated immediately.

The following morning, Maria again climbed those stairs to that room at the top, where she had left him the previous night, lying fully clothed upon the single bed. As she quietly pushed open the door, carrying a breakfast tray, Maria couldn't see him, for the bed was empty.

Softly she called his name, and detected a slight movement in the large leather chair. 'Ah, there you are. I have brought you some brea — !' She stopped abruptly in mid-sentence, and almost dropped the tray, her hand flying to her mouth to stifle a scream. For she had moved to the front of the chair now, and was stood facing him, her knuckles white and taut as she had to grip the tray with both hands to steady it, for she was trembling violently.

Thomas stared at her. 'Maria, what on earth is the matter? You look as though you have seen a ghost,' he said, his concern for her reflected in his voice

'*My God! He doesn't even know!*' she thought, as she desperately searched her mind for some kind way to tell him, and quickly realised there was none.

Valiantly she tried to compose herself. 'It — It's your hair, Thomas,' she stammered.

'My hair? What the devil do you mean, Maria?' he asked, running his fingers through the thick curls. 'It seems quite all right to me.'

On a sudden impulse Maria turned and placed his tray upon the table and then fell sobbing at his feet, clinging to him and burying her head in his lap.

Gently, he laid his hands upon her shaking shoulders. 'Maria, please stop your weeping and tell me what is troubling you,' he murmured consolingly.

She lifted her head and looked up at him, her lovely violet eyes, dark ringed and glistening wet with tears. 'Your hair, Thomas,' she began, her lips trembling. 'It is white as driven snow!'

He emitted a strange hollow laugh. 'I am not surprised my dear, considering what has happened. Is there a mirror in the room?'

With an effort, Maria hauled herself to her feet and lurched across the room towards the dressing table, then slowly retracing her steps, and with bated breath, she handed him the mirror.

Thomas held it up, and gazed long and hard at his mane of white locks, his expression never changing. Finally, he handed back the mirror to her. 'Yes Maria, you are quite correct. My hair is white.'

Maria was amazed at his cool acceptance of this devastating change in his appearance, for though no one else had ever suspected, she knew that Thomas had been inordinately proud of his golden coloured hair.

'Oh! My dearest Thomas. What kind of cruel fate is it that robs you of your entire family? Then still not satisfied, turns your beautiful golden hair completely white, all within the space of a few hours? Dear God. What is this curse, which seems to haunt the very name of Cartwright?'

Thomas uncoiled his long legs and, stretching himself, rose to his feet. He seemed to fill this small room with his immense stature. 'Come here, Maria,' he said quietly.

Willingly she succumbed to those familiar loving arms.

'Yes?' she queried, as she lifted her tear stained face to look at him. The love she felt for him at this terrible time, once again causing the hot tears to prick behind her eyelids.

He gazed down at her, and though his features were drawn and his eyes were dulled through lack of sleep, they still carried a message of love for this beautiful woman he had once rescued from a life of utter degradation, and whom he had later asked to be his wife.

'Do you remember the prophecy of that old man by the lake Maria?' he asked, his eyes locked onto hers.

'Yes dear, every single word. Why do you ask?'

'Because Maria. What that old man forecast has actually happened, and I feel ashamed when I think of how I ridiculed him and poured scorn upon his words. He said, one day I would need you, and you would be my only salvation. Well Maria, that day has come.'

He tightened his grip upon her, and suddenly it seemed to Maria as though a curtain had been raised, allowing a blinding flash of sunlight into her mundane, ordinary life. In jubilation, she almost shouted her thoughts aloud. *Thank God, he hasn't forgotten what the old man said, and now in his moment of grief and desolation, he has turned to me!*

Her heart was singing with sheer joy, but only momentarily, for her brief moment of happiness was tinged almost immediately with sadness, as she remembered the reason for her presence in this house. She roused herself from her reverie, for he was speaking again.

'And I do need you, Maria, now and forever. Please promise you will never leave me.'

Even though she was aware of the cause of his distress, and his anguished cry for help and companionship, she still thrilled to the timbre of his voice and the words he spoke.

Maria continued to gaze into those beloved eyes, as she softly replied. 'Thomas. My dearest dearest Thomas. I have no need to make any such promise. For you must know deep within your heart, I love you. I will never leave you. For I could not live without you.'

The love reaching out to him from her lovely violet eyes, shone through to his befuddled mind like a beacon of hope, and he clung to her as would a drowning man.

He seemed reassured by her words, and at last became calm and more rational in his demeanour.

'Come along Thomas. Eat your breakfast. Your tea is getting cold,' she said crisply. 'I know all this has been a tragic shock to you, my dear, but life must go on, and if poor Kate is up there somewhere watching over us, I am sure she would agree with me.'

Maria had decided to take a firmer stance with him, and though inwardly her heart was crying out for him in his hour of torment, apparently her strategy appeared to be working, for he sat down at the table and commenced eating.

When he had finished the meal, he pushed his plate away and looked at her. 'Did you say William brought you here last night?' he asked abruptly.

'Yes, and Annie.'

'Are they downstairs now Maria?' he asked, pushing back his chair and rising from the table.

'Yes. Come along, we will go down together,' she replied, gathering up the breakfast things and placing them on the tray.

He followed her down the iron spiral stairs, at the foot of which was a normal landing on the next floor, leading to a wooden staircase rising from the ground floor.

As they reached the entrance hall, they heard voices coming through a half open door, leading to a room at the front of the house.

Thomas pushed the door fully open and

walked in, followed closely by Maria. William, Annie and Bull were standing in the centre of the room, discussing the funeral arrangements with George Teanby, but the conversation ceased abruptly as Thomas and Maria entered.

The four of them stared in stunned silence at the change which had been wrought in the appearance of Thomas. However, William was the first to recover, and stepping forward he gripped the hand of his son-in-law.

'Terrible tragedy this Thomas,' he said brokenly. 'What the devil happened on the *Elizabeth Kate*, do you know?'

It was a poignant scene to behold, as the two men gripped each other in a silent embrace, welded together by their mutual pain, and a mental picture of the horror which had overwhelmed and laid waste, the lives of their loved ones.

'No, I have no idea,' replied Thomas, gently releasing his partner. 'I had a word with Charlie Butlin, but apparently he was in the village when the explosion occurred, and there are several witnesses who will testify to that.'

'Yes I know. I saw him last night. Oh! My God Thomas. I don't know if I can carry on without Lottie!' As he mentioned her name, William's voice broke, and he collapsed in the nearest chair, burying his head in his hands, his broad shoulders shaking with uncontrollable sobs.

George Teanby touched Thomas on the arm and drew him aside. 'Sorry to interrupt Thomas,' he said quietly. 'But I must get back to work. I have finished the two coffins for your children. What do you wish me to do with poor Kate's remains?'

Thomas looked at the carpenter uncomprehendingly, and then as in a dream, he remembered leaving his wife's boot, wrapped in a sheet at this man's yard.

'Please make another one, the same size as the children's. Place what remains of my wife inside, and I will have the three buried together at the village church, in a plot overlooking the confluence of the three rivers, if that is possible.'

George Teanby thanked him, and returned to his unenviable but very necessary task.

On the morning of the third day following that terrible catastrophe, the village of Watersmeet began to fill with horse drawn vehicles of every description, and though the four small shops had taken in unprecedented supplies of bread and cold meats, including many other goodies, by lunch time all their shelves had been stripped of everything that was edible or drinkable, some of the shopkeepers even resorting to emptying their own larders, revelling in this unexpected windfall of profit.

In early afternoon, the hugely assembled cortege left the tall house which William had built for his beloved Lottie, the house she had so adamantly refused to visit, and now would never see, and wound its way through the sun-splashed village streets, the mourners walking behind the horse drawn hearse towards the church.

The three hundred or so inhabitants of Watersmeet had never experienced a funeral to compare with the sheer size of this one, and the small church was quickly filled to capacity, leaving scores of people standing outside in the hot afternoon sun.

At last the service was concluded, and the pall bearers carried their pathetically small burdens to three freshly dug graves, situated as close as possible to the Western wall of the churchyard, where a glimpse of the burnt out shell of the *Elizabeth Kate*, could just be seen between two cottages overlooking the three rivers.

As the vicar ended his short graveside service by sprinkling soil upon each coffin, and pronouncing the words. '*Ashes to ashes and dust to dust*,' William would have fallen but for the strong arm of Thomas supporting him, whilst Bull, with one arm around his wife and the other around Maria, did his best to comfort the two sobbing grief stricken women.

William had asked his friend George Teanby to visit the wreck and collect some ashes from the fire, hoping that a few of Lottie's would be among them. He had then instructed George to make a casket for the ashes, and place it in the hearse, to be taken into church for the funeral service.

William was now carrying that casket, as he stepped off the ferry onto the pier at Hull, accompanied by a sombre faced Thomas, Maria, Annie and Bull.

As they walked slowly along the pier, William, who had not spoken a word since leaving Watersmeet, suddenly stopped and looked around him, as if searching for someone.

'I didn't see Charlie Butlin at the funeral. Does anyone know where he is?' he asked, scrutinising the faces of other passengers as they jostled past.

'Yes, sir. I do,' replied Bull. 'He left to catch the last ferry on Saturday night. He seemed to be in a pretty bad way regarding the accident, him being in charge an'all, but he thought somebody should get back to

115

the yard, to help run things while you and Thomas were away.'

'Good,' answered William. 'He's a sound man is Charlie. I always knew I could trust him,' and with that profound remark the small party continued on their sorrowful way towards the line of hackney carriages waiting at the end of the pier.

Thomas instructed the driver to take them straight to the shipyard of Earnshaw and Cartwright where, after dismissing the carriage, he turned to his companions. 'Harness a pony and trap from the stables, Bull, to take Maria and Annie to the cottage, and I will organise one to return William and myself to Mount Pleasant.'

'Just wait a minute!' Bull turned and retraced his steps, for he was already on his way to the stables when William's crisp command rang out.

'I think it would be a good idea if you, Annie and Maria, could possibly see your way clear to come and live with us at Mount Pleasant. There is plenty of room for us all. In fact, if you wish, you and Annie could have a whole wing of the house to yourselves.'

Annie looked at her husband, but could see he was leaving the decision to her. 'Well, thank you very much for the offer,' she began. 'But I don't know. You see, we have two boys to consider, for they both stay with us when they are ashore.'

Maria had noticed the spark of anticipation in William's sad eyes, as he broached his idea, and then the cloud of disappointment flooding his features when it was on the verge of being rejected.

She was amazed at the transformation in his appearance. He looked an old man she reflected sadly, and her heart went out to him. However, her quick, agile mind suddenly perceived a window of opportunity opening up, one which would secure a future happiness for her and Miles, far beyond her wildest dreams.

The chance to live in the same house as her first and only love once again, and she grasped it eagerly using all her feminine charm.

'Personally, I think it is a splendid idea, Mr Earnshaw,' said Maria softly. 'Obviously you two men need a woman to attend to the running of a house the size of Mount Pleasant, someone you can trust implicitly. In fact, two women would be far more sensible, and I couldn't possibly manage without you, Annie,' she said, turning and smiling sweetly at her companion, who had instantly recognised Maria's ploy, and the secret command hidden behind that sweet, subtle smile.

'Why yes. That would suit us fine,' interposed Thomas. 'Of course you will come too, Bull. I am sure if we stay together, it will help to lighten the burden of loss for us all, especially William. Please say you will come, Annie.'

Maria's companion noticed the pathos in his speech, and the pleading in his eyes, and knew she could not refuse.

'I once promised Maria I would never leave her and if she still wants me I will come, but only as her friend and companion, for neither Bull or I will accept any form of charity,' she replied, with quiet dignity.

'Charity!' expostulated Thomas. 'Nothing was further from my mind. My dear Annie, if William agrees, I am offering to you the position of housekeeper at Mount Pleasant, responsible only to Maria. With free board and lodge for yourself and your husband, plus a generous remuneration which we will negotiate later.'

Annie was overjoyed at this magnificent offer, but dare not show her elation, because of the tragic circumstances surrounding the necessity of William and Thomas having to employ a housekeeper.

Maria saw the happiness behind her

friend's eyes, which was cleverly disguised by her quiet acceptance of the offer.

'Thank you very much Mr Earnshaw, and you too Master Thomas. This is a wonderful position to offer me, and I can assure you, I shall do my very best to make myself worthy of your trust in me.'

'Does that mean you accept Annie?' asked Thomas. 'And if so, can you all please come tonight?'

The three friends looked at each other, and then Bull spoke, assuming the mantle of responsibility. 'Yes, of course, Thomas. It's at times like this you need your friends around you. I will harness up that pony and trap, and we will leave for the cottage immediately.'

Maria stayed a moment, while Annie went to help her husband, and turning to Thomas murmured softly. 'Thank you, Thomas.'

'No, Maria. It is we who should be thanking you, and please inform Annie that the two boys will be most welcome to come and stay with us, whenever they are ashore. Anyway, it will be marvellous, our son once again living under the same roof as you and I.'

Maria walked away, her heart too full for her to make any lucid reply, and though she longed to skip and dance her way to th' stables, she dare not, for she knew she must observe a sense of decorum and propriety as she left the bereaved William, and her bereaved beloved Thomas. She did, however, spontaneously lift her eyes to heaven and breathe a silent, *Thank you Kate*.

4

When William and Thomas approached Mount Pleasant, the house looked a picture of peace and tranquillity, bathed as it was in the early evening sun, and yet, as they entered that huge hall, the place seemed utterly devoid of any human occupation.

The canyons of their minds became flooded with the sounds of childish laughter, and a cheerful greeting from Kate and Lottie, but the tomb like silence of the darkened hall, proved too much for William, and with a heartbroken sob, he lurched forward towards the library door, stumbling inside and slamming it shut behind him.

Thomas hesitated, wondering if he should follow his wretchedly unhappy partner, but finally decided his presence would probably be an intrusion upon William's private grief.

As he stood there in the vast silent emptiness of the deserted hall, he detected a movement from the rear of the house, and correctly assumed the slamming of the library door had disturbed the servants.

'Good evening, Master Thomas,' greeted the butler, as he padded silently across the hall floor. 'Please accept our condolences. We are all deeply shocked by this terrible loss.'

'Thank you, Milton,' replied Thomas. 'Have someone bring in our luggage, and instruct one of the stable lads to attend to the pony and trap.'

'Very good sir.'

'Oh, and Milton. Instruct Mary to prepare two of the guest rooms. We have visitors coming this evening. A married couple and a single lady.'

As the butler silently withdrew. Thomas remembered his partner alone in the library and thought perhaps it might be prudent just to have a look in and make sure he was all right. As he quietly pushed open the door, much to his consternation the room was in total darkness, for the heavy velvet curtains were tightly drawn, completely shutting out the bright evening sunlight.

Crossing swiftly to the window, and almost falling over the outstretched legs of William in the process, Thomas flung back the curtains, flooding the room with light. He turned to see William slumped in his favourite leather chair.

'What the devil did you do that for man?' he shouted angrily.

Somewhat taken aback by the older man's

show of anger, and his inflamed attitude, Thomas was about to reply in like vein, when he suddenly realised how much William must be suffering.

'I am sorry if the light offends you,' he said sympathetically. 'But we cannot live in darkness. Neither Kate nor Lottie would wish us to, and anyway life must go on. You know that as well as I.' While he was speaking, Thomas had been pouring a fair measure of whisky into a couple of glasses.

'Here, drink this. I am sure it will help,' he said, as he handed one to William.

As the golden coloured liquid burned its way down, it didn't seem to have the desired effect, for William became more morose and melancholy, and as he drained his glass, he reached for the decanter.

'Steady William,' said Thomas sharply. 'You cannot drink whisky of this quality as though it were lemonade.'

'Why not?' blustered his partner. 'I need a drink, and anyway, it might help me to forget the past.'

'The relief will only be temporary. Also you haven't eaten all day, and you are well aware of the consequences if you continue to drink on an empty stomach. However, if you must, just have a small one and I will ring for some food.'

Thomas moved across the room and pulled the tasselled cord hanging beside the fireplace. A moment later there was a discreet knock on the library door, and the butler walked in.

'Ah, Milton, ask cook to send us some supper. Anything cold will suffice, and a pot of tea.'

'Yes, Master Thomas. Will your guests be requiring any supper when they arrive, sir?'

'Later Milton. Tell cook they will be arriving later.' The butler quietly closed the door as he left the room.

No conversation passed between the two men as they waited for their meal, for each of them was too preoccupied with his own thoughts and memories of the past, and what might have been. William stayed slumped in his chair, while Thomas stood at the window, staring out with unseeing eyes at the sun-speckled, shimmering waters of the treacherous Humber.

'Dear God,' he murmured quietly to himself. 'What is this terrible fate which hangs over me, and damns and destroys everyone I love? Yet leaves me physically unscathed to live on in utter desolation?'

But Thomas Cartwright could find no answer to his prayer, and at that moment the door opened and cook entered carrying a tray, followed closely by Mary.

'Thank you cook,' said Thomas, as they placed their trays upon the table.

She was a large, red-complexioned, buxom woman, probably in her late forties, she was also the wife of the butler, Henry Milton.

Lottie had advertised in the local paper, some five years previously, for a cook and a butler, and Mr and Mrs Milton had applied for the positions, apparently because they wished to work together. Their references had been impeccable, and they had graced the rooms, hallways and kitchens of this fine old house ever since.

'Oh! sirs, what a terrible tragedy it is like, both our dear mistresses and them two bonnie bairns, all gone in one dreadful day,' said cook in a tear jerked voice, as she lifted her apron to her red-rimmed eyes. It was obvious from their distressed appearance, that both she and Mary must have been weeping for several hours.

'There-there, Mrs Milton, don't take on so,' said William in a kindly tone. 'Somehow we must strive to carry on. We are expecting you and Mary, and the rest of the servants, to help us through this terrible time.'

The two women broke into a fresh outburst of sobbing and fled the room, each holding up their aprons to their eyes.

To help break the emotion of the moment, and for the sake of something to do, Thomas moved away from the window, and proceeded to pour tea into two large cups. Scooping plenty of sugar in, he handed one to William.

'Here. Drink this,' he said laconically, at the same time passing him a plate of sandwiches.

'Thank you, Thomas. I will drink the tea, but I can't possibly eat anything.'

'Now come along, you must eat. If you don't, you will soon be joining Aunt Lottie and my beloved Kate.'

'There's a thought,' mused William, half to himself, then in his normal voice. 'What is this life all about Thomas? We never ask to be born, yet we are put on this earth, we grow up, we work like hell to try and provide a decent life for ourselves and our loved ones. Then, in the space of a few minutes during a single afternoon, everything is gone, like so much chaff before a puff of wind.'

Thomas looked at William, and considering his own dreadful loss, it was characteristic of him that his heart went out to the older man. For he had come to look upon him, not only as a partner, but also as a father figure, and he felt so helpless as he watched him suffering so much hurt and pain.

However, Thomas was saved any further attempt to dissuade William from his apathy, and he heaved a sigh of relief as he heard the welcome sound of wheels on the gravelled drive.

Maria and her companions were taken straight to the library, while a servant unloaded their luggage and took it upstairs to their respective rooms.

The three gazed in childlike wonder at the sumptuous furnishings, and the shelves stacked high with hundreds of beautiful leather bound books. They felt shy and awkward, for none of them were accustomed to such luxurious surroundings as those displayed in abundance in this room.

Thomas immediately sensed the embarrassment of his friends and, crossing to the fireplace, once again pulled the bell cord. 'I have rung for some more tea and sandwiches,' he said casually, attempting to put them at ease. 'You must all be famished, after such a long and arduous day.'

'Yes, Thomas, we are,' replied Maria, at last breaking her silence as she realised what he was trying to do, and thought how stupid and ignorant they must have appeared to him. 'I'm sorry Thomas, but you see we three are not used to living in such luxury as this, and having just left our small cottage to come and live here, well even you must admit, it is somewhat different to say the least.'

Thomas was about to reply, when there was a light knock on the door and Mrs Milton, accompanied by Mary, came into the room carrying further supplies of food and the inevitable pot of tea.

The sound of voices and the presence of other people in the room, had aroused William from his lethargic stupor, self induced by the amount of neat whisky he had imbibed in too short a time. Emitting a slight cough to announce his return to the present, and also to attract attention, he addressed the cook.

'Ah, Mrs Milton. I wish you and Mary to be introduced to Miss Maria, for from tomorrow morning, she will be the head of all domestic affairs in this household. And Mrs Annie Hyde, the new housekeeper.' Then turning to Maria and Annie. 'Mrs Milton is the cook, her husband is the butler, and Mary is the parlour maid.'

The three women and the girl nodded to each other and then, with a quick curtsy in the direction of William, Mary and the cook returned to the kitchen.

The following morning only Bull turned up at the yard, for William paid a visit to the vicar, to discuss the problem of where and when he could inter the casket containing his late wife's ashes in the small churchyard of the village church where they were married. Whilst Thomas had decided to embark upon a long ride over the Wolds, to try and ease the pain and the empty void within his aching heart. This was not to be, however, for everywhere he went brought back vivid memories of the times, he and Kate had visited these same woods and meadows together, sometimes with the children and sometimes on their own, and this only served to enhance the hurt within him.

Finally, he allowed his horse to halt, and raising his eyes to heaven, once again cried out in anger to his God. '*Why? Why have you taken my loved ones away from me?*' he thundered. '*Damn it all. I have done nothing to deserve such vile treatment as this!*'

His cry of anguish was greeted by a deathly silence, a silence broken only by the lilting song of a skylark, high above in the clear blue sky. However, the sound only served to twist the knife still further in his heart, as he remembered that other skylark all those years ago, on just such a day as this, during their first picnic together.

He sat awhile and watched the lark as

it hovered above him, and then he envied the easy freedom with which it left all earthbound cares and woes behind, and soared with such obvious, consummate ease toward heaven, singing as though its tiny heart would burst.

At length, and with a deep sigh of loneliness and utter misery, Thomas turned wearily for home. Fortunately the horse knew which direction to take, for by now his master had become disorientated, and completely oblivious of his surroundings, though he recalled someone once telling him, *Time is a great healer*.

'Well,' he reflected aloud. 'I'm afraid it is going to take a very long time for this particular wound to heal.'

He was astounded when his horse drew up in the courtyard at the rear of Mount Pleasant, for he had no recollection of the return journey, and he was even more astounded when he glanced up at the clock above the stables, and saw the time was after five o'clock.

As the stable lad came to take his horse, Maria ran out from the rear entrance to the house. 'Where have you been all day Thomas?' she asked, a worried frown creasing her otherwise smooth honey coloured brow. 'When you didn't return for lunch, I had a horse saddled and came searching for you, but of course I never found you, so eventually I gave up. I only returned half an hour ago.'

'Well, please don't worry any more Maria, for I'm here now, safe and sound, as you can see.'

She looked at him closely. There was no laughter in those wonderful, blue eyes she had adored, from the first moment their paths had crossed. Only a drab lacklustre look, and she vowed to herself she would return them to their former brilliance, if it took the rest of her life.

'But I do worry Thomas. One hears so many strange stories, about how shock and sudden bereavement can affect those who were close.'

For the first time since the tragedy, Thomas actually smiled. 'Surely, Maria, you didn't think I was going to ride off beyond the horizon without so much as a goodbye kiss, did you?'

Her heart had warmed when she saw him smile, brief as it was. 'No of course not dearest,' she replied softly. 'But I was worried about you. I don't suppose you have eaten anything all day, have you?'

'No, and you have just reminded me how hungry I am. I will have a quick wash and

131

change, then come down for a meal.' He patted her on the cheek, and as they parted at the door, he said. 'Thank you for coming to this house, Maria, and please do not worry unduly about me. Just give me a little time and together, you and I will be able to cope with this harrowing situation.'

Maria stood transfixed, her heart beating a little faster, as she allowed her mind to assimilate his parting words. 'Oh! My darling Thomas,' she breathed softly to herself. 'My love for you will vanquish all the pain and hurt of your terrible loss, and I promise you, a year from now, peace and happiness will once again reign supreme in this household.'

After William had returned from his visit to the vicarage, he had spent the remainder of that day closeted in the library, attempting to obliterate the events of the past few days with the aid of the fast diminishing contents of a bottle of whisky.

By the time Thomas had consumed a large meal, and his hunger had once again been satiated, he made his way to the library, and much to his chagrin, found William lying back in his chair, apparently in a drunken stupor, the empty whisky bottle on the floor beside him. Crossing swiftly to the fireplace, he gave a sharp pull on the bell rope, and almost immediately Mary appeared in the doorway.

'Have Miss Maria, come and see me at once,' he said curtly. Minutes later there was a tap on the door, and Maria walked in. 'Did you know William was at home?' he asked abruptly.

Her expression changed when she saw the mood he was in. 'Yes of course. He came back before noon, and said he was going to sit in the library, so I sent a tray of sandwiches in and he informed Mary, he didn't wish to be disturbed.'

It was at that moment her gaze fell upon the motionless figure of William, reclining in a somnolent position in his favourite chair. Her face paled. 'Good heavens, Thomas. Is he dead?' she asked, a tremor in her voice

'No, my dear. Just dead drunk,' he replied grimly.

There was a further knock on the door and Annie came in, followed by her husband, who had just returned from the yard. Bull couldn't help but smile, when he saw the sprawling figure of William. However, his smile quickly disappeared as Thomas spoke.

'This may look funny to you, Bull, but I can assure you it is deadly serious,' he said caustically. 'I think we could have quite a problem here. Apparently William is hell bent on drowning his sorrow and loneliness with the aid of this.' He aimed a vicious kick at the empty bottle, and sent it flying across the room, as though to add impetus to his words. 'And he will probably destroy himself in the process,' he added disparagingly.

Annie was the first to recover after this emotional outburst. 'But what can we do, Master Thomas. For, after all, he is the master of this house, and woe betide any of us if we try to take the whisky away from him, or even attempt to hide it.'

'Yes, I appreciate that Annie,' replied Thomas in a calmer tone. 'I'm afraid there isn't much any of us can do if William is determined to follow this degrading downhill course. Anyway, I will take him upstairs now and try to convince him of the error of his ways in the morning.'

Thomas did not, however, succeed in his efforts to persuade his elder partner to ease up on his drinking. In fact, the habit grew steadily worse, and after intermittent visits to the yard on only two or three days a week, he finally decided to stay at home, and spend his time drinking in the library, with the casket containing Lottie's ashes, on the small table beside his chair.

For William had decided not to have the casket interred, but to keep it with him at

Mount Pleasant until, as he phrased it, 'my time comes, and then we will be buried together!'

Maria had been passing the library door, when she heard him saying those very words, and after knocking lightly had walked in. 'Sorry, Mr Earnshaw,' she said, rather embarrassed. 'I thought I heard you speaking to someone.'

'Aye. You did that, lass,' he replied, and though his words were slightly slurred, he seemed quite sober. 'I was just telling Lottie here,' he gently stroked the casket. 'I am keeping her here waiting for me, and then we will go together.'

Maria eyed him with some trepidation. 'Do you think that is wise, sir? I mean, aren't you being rather morbid?'

William half raised himself from his chair, his features horribly contorted, his eyes wild and staring. 'Wise? Morbid? Who the devil do you think you are, to advise me on what is wise, when you are just a miserable skivvy and I am the master of this house? Go on woman, get out of this room now, before I throw you out!'

Maria was astounded at the sudden change in his attitude towards her and, though more than a little frightened, she still felt sorry for him as she quickly withdrew. For she knew this was not the real William Earnshaw talking, but some vile ghastly monster he had unwittingly created, through his over indulgence in that horrible soul destroying demon lurking within those bottles of whisky.

Maria awaited the return of Thomas from the yard with growing impatience and, when he at last arrived, half an hour later than usual, she met him in the hall and, taking him by the arm, marched him quite forcefully into the drawing room.

He was immediately aware by her tight lipped expression and her actions, that something was drastically wrong. 'What on earth is the matter, Maria?'

She told him of her unpleasant encounter with William earlier that day, and stamping her tiny foot, swore she would never enter the library again while William was still in there.

Thomas could see she had worked herself up into a real state, but privately thought the whole mess was just a storm in a tea cup. He did however, cross to the bell rope and give it a gentle pull.

Promptly, there was a light tap on the door, and Mary came in.

'Ah, Mary. Send Milton to see me.'

The maid turned and left, silently closing the door and almost immediately there was a further, more masculine knock upon the old oak panels, and the butler entered the room.

'Milton,' began Thomas, going straight to the crux of the problem, as was his wont, with no meandering preliminaries. 'Earlier today, Miss Maria experienced a rather nasty scene with Mr Earnshaw, and I am assigning to you the task of being Mr Earnshaw's personal valet, to take effect immediately.'

'Yes, sir. Will that be a promotion or a demotion, sir?' asked Milton impassively.

'Dammit man, neither,' snapped Thomas. 'With the help of your good wife, and the advent of Miss Maria and Mrs Hyde, I think we have sufficient staff to cope with your duties for a while.'

'Excuse me, sir, but how long is this duty likely to last?'

It became obvious Thomas was quickly losing his patience with what he saw as totally unnecessary and irrelevant questions. 'I have no idea, Milton. Just as long as Mr Earnshaw requires your services.' He indicated the interview was at an end and, pointedly ignoring Maria, the butler gave a muttered, 'Thank you, sir,' and left the room.

'I think I may have just made my first enemy,' murmured Maria, as the door closed upon the retreating figure of Milton.

'Please do not worry about him Maria. You cannot possibly hold yourself responsible for William's indiscretions. No, the blame lies entirely with him and his stupid drinking. Anyway you were quite right in reporting the incident to me, and I fervently hope he quickly resolves his drink problem, and this household can then return to some form of normality.'

However, William did not resolve his drink problem, and after several weeks of this self-inflicted, destructive debauchery, it became apparent to Thomas, as junior partner in the firm of Earnshaw and Cartwright, that dramatic action was needed, to prevent the business sliding into bankruptcy. For he was unable to make vital major decisions without the aid of his senior partner, and one or two important customers began slipping away to some of their more avaricious and envious competitors.

Finally, in desperation, Thomas paid a visit to their solicitor, which resulted in him calling at Mount Pleasant early the following morning, armed with a document for William to sign, giving Thomas the Power of Attorney over the shipyard, the farms, and any other business enterprise accredited to the name of William Earnshaw, including the wine

138

merchants in London.

Much to the surprise of Thomas and his legal aid, they had no difficulty in persuading William to sign the document, and thereby relinquish his hold upon the reins of authority. In fact, he seemed to be thankful to be rid of the responsibility, and hinted as much, when he poured each of them a drink to celebrate, what he called, 'My early retirement from the centre of shipbuilding and commercial life in the town of Kingston-upon-Hull,' adding happily, and with a demeanour which promised a hard day's drinking ahead, as he drained his glass, 'This is the first one today.'

The whole procedure had been completed quite amicably and, within half an hour of his arrival, the solicitor was once again seated in his trap, heading towards Hull.

After Thomas had seated himself firmly at the helm, trade began to improve almost immediately, and those customers who, like rats, had deserted what they thought to be a sinking ship, came scuttling back with hang dog expressions and lame excuses, for they knew where they could be sure of quality workmanship. Apart from the fact that Thomas had built up quite a reputation along the river, for his honesty and integrity in business, and the use of his fists to help any smaller man, in a fight which he did not consider to be fair.

The only speck on the horizon at the yard of Earnshaw and Cartwright during this era of expanding trade and mounting profits, apart from William of course, was the maudlin melancholy figure of Charlie Butlin.

The loss of the *Elizabeth Kate* and all those on board, seemed to have affected Charlie more than anyone. He also had turned to drink. This however, had no derogatory effect upon his work rate, not that is until one afternoon when Thomas walked into one of the large warehouses and found Charlie embroiled in a drunken brawl with a fellow carpenter.

He simply walked between the two fighting men, grabbed each one by the scruff of his neck, and banged their heads together. There was no gasp of astonishment from the score or so men who had gathered to watch the fight, for most of them had seen Thomas in action before, and this was his normal method of dealing with any of his recalcitrant employees.

Stepping over the prostrate bodies, he addressed the men. 'Now get back to work.' Though he spoke calmly, there was no mistaking the note of authority in his voice and, looking rather sheepish, the men silently filed past him.

Walt the foreman had followed Thomas into the building, and was now standing beside him.

'Ah, Walt. When Butlin recovers, bring him to me in the office.'

'Yes, Master Thomas,' replied Walt, with what sounded like relief in his voice.

Some time later, a sullen, dishevelled Charlie Butlin was shown into the office. 'Thank you, Walt. You may go now,' said Thomas without looking up.

When they were alone, he closed the ledger he had been studying and, raising his head, looked at Charlie with those soul searching, piercing blue eyes.

'You may sit down, Charlie,' he said kindly. However, the man remained standing, if possible looking more sullen and abrasive than before. 'All right, Butlin, now what is this all about?' asked Thomas, a note of steel creeping into his voice.

Charlie remained silent.

'Now look here, Butlin. I have heard of your night time drinking orgies, but have never mentioned it before because, prior to this incident today, you have refrained from allowing it to affect your work. I also know that, previous to that tragic accident at Watersmeet, you were a hard working and conscientious tradesman. Since then, however, for reasons known only to yourself, you have allowed your life to go to pieces. I cannot understand your sullen attitude toward your fellow man. You can't blame yourself for what happened. In fact, you were completely exonerated at the inquest. So, is there something else which you are keeping from me?'

Still there was no reply, as Charlie remained passively resentful.

'Very well, Butlin, if you can put forward no excuse for your unreasonable behaviour, I have no alternative but to send you out tonight on board the *Sea Hawk* as ship's carpenter. At least that should help to cure you of any drink problem you may have.'

For the first time Charlie deigned to speak. '*The Sea Hawk*! As ship's carpenter?' he echoed, in an aggrieved tone. 'William would never have treated me like this.'

His employer's patience was beginning to wear thin. 'I presume by 'William,' you are referring to Mr Earnshaw,' he snapped. 'Well, he isn't here, but I am and I can assure you, Charlie Butlin, I have Mr Earnshaw's full authority to run this yard as I see fit. Now if you have nothing more to say, consider this interview at an end.'

One cold January day, some three months after Charlie had left these shores, Thomas and Bull were just entering the yard gates, after enjoying a hot lunch, when a sweating horse slithered to a halt beside them.

'Beg y' pardon, Master Thomas,' panted the rider, without even bothering to dismount. 'Miss Maria says to come home quick!'

'What is it, John. What's the trouble?' asked Thomas, recognising the youth as one of the grooms from Mount Pleasant

'I don't rightly know sir, but I think it's something to do with Mr Earnshaw like.'

Thomas spoke over his shoulder, for he was already on his way to the stables. 'See that horse is given a good rub down Bull, and fix that lad up with a fresh one.'

It seemed only seconds later he was riding past them. 'You are in charge now, Bull,' he shouted, as he galloped out of the yard.

Maria was standing at the front entrance waiting for him. He could see by her expression and pallid features, that something terrible had happened. Leaping off his lathered mount, almost before it had stopped, he dashed up the steps towards her. 'What is it, Maria? Has something happened to William?'

'Oh! My dearest Thomas. How glad I am you have come. Yes, William is dead!'

143

Her last words were barely above a whisper, as she collapsed sobbing in his arms. Picking her up, as he would a child, Thomas carried her indoors and through the hall to the warmth of the drawing room, where he lay her gently down upon the sofa. As he gazed down at her pale face in the quiet stillness of this lovely room, something stirred within him. A passion, and a fire which had lain dormant since Kate's untimely death.

Now, however, the sheer beauty of her had rekindled the flame of his love for her, and he promised himself, even at that moment, in this house stalked by the Grim Reaper, that he would make up to her for all those years she had lost.

While he was silently admiring her beauty, untouched as it was, by the cares suffered by the majority of her contemporaries, her long black lashes slowly lifted, revealing those lovely, languid violet eyes.

He caught his breath as he felt his loins begin to stir, and Maria, now with her eyes wide open, saw the look of desire and adoration in the eyes of the man she loved, and a frisson of pure pleasure rippled down the length of her spine.

Frantically, they began to rip off their clothes, as though the world would end in the next two minutes, and they would have no time to complete this long awaited reunion.

Now, almost naked, Maria suddenly stopped. 'What about William?' she panted, her body flushed and trembling with anticipation of what was to come.

Thomas, in the act of unbuckling his belt, continued to let it fall, and with a wry smile replied. 'He will have to wait my darling. Anyway, he's not going anywhere.'

So, Thomas and his Maria, bodies and limbs inextricably entwined, rolled naked together on the floor of the drawing room, revelling in the unbridled passion and freedom of their reborn love. Whilst William, deserted and alone, lay on his bed in the darkened room above, totally oblivious of the erotic shenanigans taking place beneath him, and all the while becoming colder and more rigid by the minute.

When the two lovers had finally slaked their mutual sexual thirst, and were once again dressed and seated, deliriously happy in their new found love, Thomas kissed her, then rose to his feet, and crossing the room, pulled upon the bell rope.

A moment later, following a subdued tap on the door, Mary entered the room.

'Bring Miss Maria and I some tea and cakes please, Mary,' said Thomas, finding it very difficult to restrain his ebullient mood, as he addressed the sad faced tear stained parlour maid.

'We shall have to try and act normally for a few days, Maria,' he said as Mary closed the door.

She looked up at him with a dazzling smile. 'For a few days? What happens then my darling?' she murmured demurely.

'I will tell you what happens then, you little witch. I shall move my things into your room, and we shall sleep together as man and wife, like we used to in the old days.'

Maria could hardly contain her happiness, and leaping to her feet, rushed into his arms. 'Oh! My dearest Thomas, that will be wonderful,' she cried ecstatically, as once again their lips met in a searing lovers' kiss.

And that was how a shocked Mary found them, locked together in an embrace which left nothing to the imagination, as she gently pushed open the door, carrying a laden tray.

'Oh! I do beg pardon, sir,' she stammered, blushing profusely. 'But I couldn't knock, sir, on account of the tray.'

'That's quite all right, Mary,' replied Thomas nonchalantly, still holding Maria, though not quite so tightly. 'I was just trying to comfort Miss Maria in this hour of sadness. Please put the tray on the table.'

As Maria lifted her tear filled eyes to look at the maid, Mary almost dropped the tea things, for she was so taken aback by what she had seen, she had forgotten all about the tray. However, that little charade didn't fool Mary for one moment, and she could hardly wait to get back to the kitchen to tell the others of her discovery.

'They didn't fool me, even if they think they did,' she blurted out, as she closed the kitchen door.

'Whatever are you babbling on about Mary?' asked cook, as she carefully placed her mug of tea upon the white scrubbed table top.

'Them two. Master Thomas and Miss Maria. I walked into the drawing room and there they was, right in the middle of the room. Kissing and canoodling like a couple of sweethearts!'

'They wasn't?' said cook in a shocked voice. 'Why that's disgusting like, and him laying upstairs hardly cold. I really don't know what things are coming to, that I don't. What do you think Mr Milton?'

The butler had been sitting at the table, smiling smugly to himself, for he was very thankful to be relieved of the odious, unenviable task of answering to every whim of his late master. 'Oh, stop thee mithering woman. You can't expect a fine upstanding gentleman like Master Thomas to live the life of a monk. Anyway, I can't say as I blame him, I wouldn't mind having a go at that Miss Maria meself.'

'Now that's enough, James Milton!' snapped his wife. 'We don't want any talk like that in my kitchen.' Then, turning to Mary. 'And you'd best keep this to yourself young lady, if you want to keep your job.'

It was a sad reflection upon the life and times of William Earnshaw, that none of his servants mourned his passing. For in recent months they had become utterly demoralised and completely disenchanted by his incessant drinking, and continual pulling on that damn bell rope, summoning one or other of their number to his room, only to be met by a torrent of drunken abuse, or some well aimed missile hurled from the bed, usually in the form of an empty whisky bottle.

None of them that is, with the exception of Mary, but she was a very emotional soul, and no one took any notice of her. For she had been known to burst into tears on more than one occasion at the sight of one of the household cats carrying a bird in its mouth, or even a mouse.

Thomas learned later that evening that William had consumed more than his usual share of his favourite tipple before staggering up to his bed the previous night and, when Milton went to his room in the morning, he had been unable to wake him.

Maria had immediately summoned the doctor, but some three hours had elapsed before he arrived. After the doctor had examined William, he came downstairs and handed Maria the death certificate, stating that William had died from a massive stroke exacerbated by his uninhibited appetite for more alcohol.

Three days later, William was laid to rest in the same village churchyard where he and Lottie were married, and the casket containing what he had believed to be her ashes, was buried with him.

Very few people attended his funeral for, in the six months prior to his death, William had virtually become a recluse because of his excessive drinking, and consequently the majority of his friends from earlier days had gradually drifted away.

One couple who were faithful to the end however, were old Joe and his wife from the country inn. After the funeral, the family solicitor went over to Joe and asked if he and his wife would accompany the remaining members of the cortege to Mount Pleasant, for the reading of the will.

Well, of course, neither of them was expecting anything from William's estate, and were all agog with excitement as they entered the library, along with Thomas and the others.

As the reading of *The Last Will and Testament Of William Earnshaw* continued, it transpired that he had left his share of the inn to the innkeeper and his wife. One hundred pounds each to Mr and Mrs Milton and one hundred pounds to Mary. There was also the sum of Two hundred and fifty pounds each, to Walt, (his faithful foreman at the shipyard) his estate manager, and also to Maria and Mr and Mrs Hyde for their unstinting help and companionship in these troubled times.

Thomas Cartwright ('Whom I have come to look upon as my own son') inherited the bulk of the estate, including the house and all its contents, the stables and the horses, the shipyard and the farms, all the properties situated in the town of Kingston-upon-Hull, and the large wine merchants in the City of London.

The sounds of pleasure, and gasps of astonishment from his attentive captive audience, which greeted each individual name as the solicitor read them out, were many and varied, and, when he finally folded the document and returned it to his case, everyone began talking at once.

'Fancy the old buzzard leaving me and Mrs Milton all that,' chortled Milton.

'Whatever am I going to do with so much money?' wailed Mary. 'That lot comes to four years wages!'

Annie and her husband, were hugging each other with glee, and old Joe stomped around his wife, while even Walt and the estate manager were shaking hands, and actually laughing aloud.

The vicar and solicitor stared aghast at this unprecedented scene until Thomas, seeing the look of horror and condemnation upon their patriarchal faces, brought his fist down upon the table, and in a voice of simulated anger called the company to order.

'Ladies and Gentlemen please remember where you are,' he thundered. 'Remember also, we have only just returned from the funeral of your late employer, my partner and father-in-law and, even though you may all be overjoyed by your quite unexpected windfall, please try and bring a little propriety to this extremely sad occasion.'

In the silence which followed his outburst, Thomas turned to Maria. 'Now, my dear. Do

I remember you mentioning something about food for our guests?' he asked quietly.

'Yes, of course, I had completely forgotten in all the excitement. Annie. Cook. Mr Milton. Mary, please lead the way to the dining room.'

Annie and the servants instantly complied, and the others, all looking rather sheepish, silently followed them, leaving Thomas and Maria alone.

For seconds only, their eyes locked, then she was in his arms. 'Oh! My darling Thomas. At last all this is your . . . '

He silenced her with his lips as they met her own, in a hungry passionate kiss, closing his eyes to the outside world, as the heady perfume of her luxuriant black tresses, assailed his senses.

Finally tearing himself away. 'Maria! Maria!' he gasped. 'For God's sake. Not now, not while the house is full of people. You really must try to curb your insatiable appetite.'

She laughed, a happy bubbling chuckle, as she patted her crumpled dress and looked up at him adoringly with her lovely violet eyes. 'I know Thomas, I know, but isn't it just wonderful, to allow it to run out of control occasionally?'

He turned her round and slapped her

bottom. 'Now get along with you to the dining room, you little hussy, before I carry you upstairs.'

'Ooh, yes please, Master!' she flung at him, as she ran out of the room.

5

The prosperity of Kingston-upon-Hull as a major port, had at first floundered with the advent of the railway. Eventually however, the Merchants, Shipbuilders and Trawler Owners realised their full potential, sending train loads of fresh fish to the industrial centres of the North.

As a direct result of the railway phenomenon, the shipyard of Earnshaw and Cartwright continued to prosper. For the trains not only took out fish, but brought into the docks wagons loaded with every type of commodity desired by the heavily populated, fast growing cities on the Continent of Europe, culminating in the build up of a huge export market through the port.

The shipyard was well placed to take full advantage of this boom in expanding world trade, and the stocks in the yard were fully occupied by the building of new ships.

Sometimes, during a rare, quiet moment, Thomas Cartwright would pause and wonder if all this good fortune was too good to be true, and think perhaps the terrible fate which had followed him throughout his life, had at last lifted the curse from his shoulders, when suddenly, though indirectly and without warning, she struck again.

Soon after William's funeral, Thomas had initiated the building of a new steam yacht, larger and faster than her predecessor the *Elizabeth Kate*, to be named *The Maria* and now, two years later, she was finished, and had only recently returned from her maiden voyage.

It was in the summer of that year, during a lull in the work rate at the yard, Thomas decided to take Maria, her companion and her husband, on a cruise down to the South Coast for a three weeks' holiday.

The Maria had a full complement of crew on board, including ship's cook and engineer, and Mary also accompanied them as Maria's personal maid. Consequently, Maria and Annie had very little to do, except eating, sleeping and sightseeing, or making themselves look as beautiful and attractive as possible.

On the evening of their return, as they tied up at the private landing stage below Mount Pleasant, they all enthused about what a wonderful holiday it had been, and of how they must repeat it again sometime in the near future.

Thomas organised a couple of men from

the house to help with the offloading of their trunks, and then instructed the captain to sail *The Maria* back to her moorings at the yard.

The following morning Thomas and Bull rode into the shipyard, sun bronzed and fit, and eager to start work on an apparent backlog of orders which had built up during their absence.

After leafing through the pile of documents littering his desk, Thomas sent for Walt, only to be told by an agitated youth that the yard foreman had been killed in an accident at work some two weeks ago. He listened in dismay as the young man told how Walt had been found in the hold of a cargo ship, crushed beneath a heavy crate but, when the doctor was called he said the foreman had been dead for three or four hours.

As the youth was leaving, Miles came into the office. 'Hello father, it's good to see you back safe and sound.'

Father and son greeted each other in an affectionate embrace, for since the loss of his other children, Thomas had become very close to his first born.

'Thank you, son, and I must give you a word of praise for running the yard so efficiently while we were away. Now what is this I hear about Walt being killed in an accident?'

156

However, Miles could only reiterate what the youth had told him. 'By the way father. There's a message for you. I attended Walt's funeral because I thought it my duty, if only to represent you and the yard. Anyway, when it was over, his widow came to me, and asked if I would inform you she wishes to see you immediately you return.'

Thomas knocked tentatively on the door of this tiny terrace house filled with sadness, wondering what he could say to comfort the widow in her distress, but at the same time filled with curiosity over this apparently urgent summons.

A middle aged, small neat woman opened the door, and her care worn features broke into a welcoming smile, as she recognised her stalwart visitor.

'Good morning, Mrs Ackroyd,' said Thomas politely. 'I understand you wish to see me.'

'Aye, that I do, Master Thomas. Please come in, only mind your head. These places weren't built for strapping young fellas like you.'

Thomas bowed his head as instructed, and followed her into the house, to find to his surprise that he was already in the front room, for the door opened straight onto the street.

'Now sit yourself down sir, and I'll bring

you a nice cup of tea and a piece of cake.'

Before he could remonstrate, she had disappeared through, what he correctly assumed to be the kitchen door, so he sat back and surveyed the room and, though it was small and cheaply furnished, everything was neat and spotlessly clean.

He was reflecting how perfectly this room resembled its owner, when the widow reappeared, carrying a large cup of tea, and a plate containing a huge slice of cake.

Placing them on the small table beside his chair, she said. 'There you are sir,' then, thrusting her hand in some secret fold of her dress, she withdrew a long brown envelope. 'And here's the letter my poor Walt left, addressed to you sir.'

'Ah yes. Please accept my condolences, and do not hesitate to let me know if there is anything I can do to help.'

A single tear trickled down the widow's cheek. 'No, thank you very much, sir for, as you know, old Mr Earnshaw, God rest his soul, left us very well provided for. Now you sit back, Master Thomas, enjoy your tea and read my Walt's letter, I have plenty to do in the kitchen.'

When he was alone, Thomas had a sip of his tea, then proceeded to open the envelope, to reveal two sheets of closely printed words, executed in a stumbling uneducated hand.

To Master Thomas.

When you read this letter I shall be dead. Charlie Butlin has tried to kill me twice and this time he has done it. You know he has been drinking a lot lately. Well, one night I met him in a pub and he got blind drunk. He started telling me about the Elizabeth Kate and how he set the fire in that Russian ship by laying a fuse across a saucer holding a lighted candle.

He did that on the Friday night knowing that when the candle burnt down and started the fire next morning somebody would send for Mr Earnshaw. Well, as you know, that's what happened like, leaving Charlie in charge of the Elizabeth Kate.

He had eight sticks of dynamite hidden in a room where he used to live and, after Mr Earnshaw had left to help fight the fire, Charlie fetched the dynamite and took it aboard the ship. When he dropped anchor below Watersmeet, he killed Jim the apprentice with a hammer, also Mrs Earnshaw. He smothered your two lovely kids and left them on deck then went below and forced your poor Kate to strip before having his way with her. He even laughed when he told me he couldn't get her boots off. Then he chained her to the boiler and the dynamite to some pipes before setting a fuse to a bit of candle. Just enough to give him time to reach the village. The next morning he remembered telling me all this and said if I told anybody he would kill me. I am very sorry Master Thomas. I should have said something before.

Anyway you know now so I leave the murdering bastard in your hands.

When he went to Australia and Sam adopted him, the adoption people couldn't read old Sam's writing and they mistook the last two letters of Charlie's name to be IN instead of ER. You see his name isn't Butlin. It is Butler!

Yes, he is Jed Butler's bastard son and somehow he found out who killed his old man and all that fornicating and murdering was his revenge.

Goodbye Master Thomas. It has been good knowing and working for you.

Your faithful servant,
Walter Ackroyd.

Thomas sat a long time in that quiet room, stunned by the revelations of this letter from the grave, the silence only broken intermittently by the passing traffic on the street outside.

The knuckles of his huge fist were taut and white as he gripped Walt's damning missive,

160

and as he reread it a dozen times, the thought of how his beautiful Kate and lovely innocent children must have suffered at the hands of that psychopathic rapist and murderer were almost too much to bear.

One positive thought did begin to emerge however, from the heaving chaos screaming through his tortured mind, which caused all others to pale into insignificance.

He must find and kill Charlie Butler!

So preoccupied was he with this single thought of how to formulate a plan to seek out and totally destroy the fiend who had annihilated his entire family, Thomas failed to hear the widow return.

'Master Thomas,' she repeated, a little louder the second time, and Thomas looked up, startled. 'I do beg pardon sir, but I thought you must have dropped off like.'

'No, Mrs Ackroyd. I was in deep thought and didn't hear you come in,' he replied, hurriedly folding the letter and thrusting it into his jacket pocket.

The widow never asked what was in her late husband's letter. She seemed more concerned about the tea she had brought for her guest, and Thomas didn't volunteer any information on the matter.

'Oh, Master Thomas. You haven't finished your tea, nor even touched that lovely piece of cake. Sit still and I will brew a fresh pot.'

'Please don't bother. I am sorry about the cake, but I shall have to be going now.' Thomas replied, as he eased himself out of the chair and walked towards the door. 'Goodbye, Mrs Ackroyd, and thank you for seeing me.'

He made an unnecessarily hasty exit, only just remembering in time to lower his head, in order to avoid the door lintel. Though seething inwardly, his manner was cold and calculating as he passed through the gateway of the shipyard, beneath the sign bearing his name, and he strode purposefully across the yard, straight towards the stairs leading to his office.

Miles and Bull were standing in the office discussing some foreign ship's manifest as Thomas entered, and they both knew immediately someone was in very big trouble. 'Leave us Miles,' he said curtly.

Miles was on the point of replying when he caught the glint in his father's eye, thought better of it, and decided it was time to go.

When they were alone, Thomas produced Walt's letter and flung it down on the desk. 'Read that!' he said harshly.

Without speaking, his friend picked up the letter, removed it from the envelope and proceeded to read, while Thomas paced around the confines of the office like a caged animal. Finally, Bull slowly folded the letter and replaced it in its envelope, his features a mixture of anger and disbelief.

'Well the scheming little rat!' he ejaculated at last. 'Fancy, all that time he was worming his way into William's favour, he was planning his revenge, to murder both your wives and your children. I saw that fight you had with Jed Butler and he asked for everything he got. He started it like he always did, and the fact he was killed was a pure accident.'

'Yes Bull, I agree,' replied Thomas quietly. 'Though apparently Charlie Butler doesn't.'

'So, what are we going to do about him, Thomas?'

For a further few minutes Thomas continued his pacing, his brow puckered in deep thought, when suddenly he stopped, and bringing his fist down upon his open palm, turned to his friend. 'Find me a copy of the ship's manifest that Butler is on.'

Bull quickly searched through the files, and handed one to Thomas.

'Ah, this is it,' he said triumphantly, as he leafed through the file. 'He evidently docked just after we went on holiday, and sailed to Lisbon last week. That would allow him ample time to get rid of Walt, and make his death look like an accident, but of course he hadn't reckoned on poor old Walt having previously written this letter to me.'

A new note of urgency crept into his voice. 'Right Bull, have *The Maria* refuelled and a fresh supply of stores taken on board. We sail tomorrow night!'

'What shall I do about the crew?' asked Bull, unable to hide his excitement, or his eternal zest for more adventure.

'We will take the same cook and engineer we had with us on holiday, but only two crew, and I want you to turn *The Maria* around as quickly as you can, but if possible without any apparent urgency. Also, remember Bull, all the crew must be sworn to secrecy, so be very careful whom you choose.'

'Aye aye, Cap'n,' answered Bull happily, failing miserably in his attempt to show how much he appreciated the seriousness of the situation.

Thomas allowed himself a faint smile at his friend's exuberance. 'Right, my friend, I will leave the preparations for this voyage in your capable hands, while I try to catch up on some office work, during the short time I have left before we sail.'

That evening, Thomas took Walt's missive home with him and, after dinner when they had retired to the drawing room, he produced the letter and spread it out for Maria and Annie to read.

During the reading they emitted various feminine sounds of Oohs and Ahs, but when they had read it, they were both equally vociferous in their condemnation of Charlie Butler, and in their demands for vengeance.

Consequently, there were no protestations from the two women, when Thomas told them of his plan, and that he and Annie's husband would be sailing on board *The Maria* tomorrow evening, to seek out and destroy that 'villainous murdering scum!'

Two weeks later, *The Maria* slipped into a quiet cove formed by the River Tagus, just to the North of Lisbon, and Thomas knew it was impossible for anyone to see her from any ship, anchored in or near the city docks.

Notwithstanding the habitual coolness with which Thomas confronted any dangerous situation, an air of excitement pervaded their cabin, as he and Bull prepared themselves for a night's reconnaissance up the Tagus, in the ship's rowing boat.

As they rowed silently along with muffled oars, the lights began to flicker on in the city and on several ships in the harbour, and those tied up in the docks. They weaved unnoticed through the plethora of large sailing ships, drifting ever closer to the dock wall, when Thomas suddenly spoke in a low whisper. '*There she is!*'

Bull's gaze followed the silhouette of his friend's pointing finger. 'Yes, you're right. I would recognise her anywhere, with her two tall masts and that high pointed prow.'

They rowed their small craft to within an oar's length of the ship's side, then silently glided past her, continuing upriver until finally pulling towards the shore, and beaching the boat just below 'Black Horse Square,' so called by the English, because of the magnificent equestrian statue cast in bronze, standing right in the centre of the square.

During his frequent visits to Portugal, Thomas had learned to love this land of sunshine and rivers, and more particularly the open friendliness of the Portuguese, for he had soon discovered that an English ship or an English sailor was always made most welcome.

He had come to look upon Lisbon as his favourite capital city, and he was as well acquainted with the city streets, as those of his native Hull. He also knew that, whenever Charlie Butler was berthed in some foreign port, he came ashore every evening to drink his fill of the cheap local wine in some sleazy back street tavern.

There were four streets leading to the city from Black Horse Square, with the two main ones in the centre of the uniform arcaded buildings, forming that side of the square, opposite the Tagus.

Thomas had worked out that one of these would be the most likely route Charlie would take on his return to *The Sea Hawk* and, bearing this in mind, he and Bull positioned themselves in the shadows, beneath the massive stone arches, where they could easily keep watch on all four streets leading from the city.

Occasionally, a lone Portuguese sailor would amble by, wishing them a friendly 'Boa-Noite,' as he passed, and they were beginning to wonder if their vigil had been in vain, for approximately three hours had elapsed when, on the still night air, they heard a drunken, raucous voice singing a bawdy sailor's shanty, and they both immediately recognised the voice of Charlie Butler!

Calm and relaxed, the two friends awaited the arrival of their unsuspecting victim. He was so drunk however, and so intent upon his singing, he never even noticed them as he staggered past.

Swiftly and silently they came up behind him, each taking an arm. 'Evening, Mr Butler,' said Thomas quietly, as he tightened his grip. 'Been for a drink, have you?'

Charlie looked startled as he peered at each of them in turn. 'What the hell are you two doing here?' he slurred. 'And why the devil did you call me Butler, when you know my name's Butlin.'

'Ah, but it isn't Charlie. You see we know who you really are, and why you set the fire on that Russian ship and, before you ask us how we know, Walt told us!' replied Thomas grimly.

Charlie struggled and squirmed in a vain effort to free himself from the vice like grip on each of his arms, but to no avail, and realising how futile this was, he attempted to lash out with his feet. However, Thomas and Bull simply lifted him clear of the ground and quickly carried him down to where they had beached their boat.

There is nothing like fear to clear a man's head of the effects of alcohol and by this time Charlie Butler was really scared. 'How the hell could Walt tell you, he's dead?' he shouted, with a final show of bravado.

They flung him face down on the beach and, while Thomas held both his hands behind him, Bull brought a length of rope and expertly tied Charlie's wrists together. He then produced another length and proceeded to tie his feet in the same efficient manner.

'What the hell do you think you're doing?' screamed Charlie, thoroughly terror stricken, and mouthing filthy expletives.

'We are going to drop you overboard, you scum, right in the middle of this river,' replied Thomas grimly.

Charlie began slavering at the mouth, his eyes dilated with sheer terror. 'No, you can't,' he screamed. 'What have I ever done to you?'

Thomas smashed a knotted iron hard fist into the man's side, cracking at least two of his ribs. 'What have you ever done to me?' he snarled. 'You bastard son of a no good father!'

Charlie began to whine in pain and fear, but his captors showed no pity.

'That was for my two children,' rasped Thomas. 'And this is for my wife,' he continued, as he dealt another crushing blow to his helpless victim's other side, and Charlie screamed in agony as more of his ribs caved in.

'Why don't you knock him out Thomas? At least he would be quiet,' said Bull, thinking his friend had meted out sufficient punishment to a man who was going to die anyway.

'Not likely. I need him to remain conscious. I want him to suffer as he made Kate suffer, and if his screaming bothers you, shove something in that cesspit of a mouth.'

'No, you can't. You stupid ignorant sods, you don't know who my . . . ' Charlie's last words on this earth, were cut off in mid sentence, as Bull thrust a filthy oily rag into his mouth, tying it there with a length of thin rope, thus effectively gagging him.

'Now, let's have the chain,' said Thomas coldly, unyielding in his quest for revenge upon this monster, who had obliterated his entire family. Bull brought the length of heavy anchor chain they had previously stowed in the boat, and stretched it out upon the beach. Then after tying the first link to one of Charlie's boots, they proceeded to roll him along the length of chain, until finally he was completely encased from head to toe, like some ancient Egyptian mummy, except that Charlie was wrapped in heavy, old rusty iron chain.

Then, having to use a considerable amount of their combined strength, for the body complete with chain, must have weighed at least five hundredweight, they heaved him gently into the rowing boat. Gently, not

170

because of any compassion they may have felt towards Charlie, but simply because they had no wish to smash the bottom of their boat. The two friends then pushed their small craft containing the terrified trussed up body of Charlie Butler down to the water, leaping on board as soon as it began to float.

The night was calm and clear, with just sufficient light from a half moon to enable the intrepid co-conspirators to see both banks of the river, and when they reached the middle, Bull ceased rowing.

Silently the two friends hoisted the terrific weight of Charlie's chain covered body from the bottom of the boat, and with a tremendous effort, heaved it overboard. As he disappeared beneath the black chill waters of the Tagus, Thomas, with uncharacteristic relish, shouted down to the inky depths below. *'Goodbye Charlie Butler, you bastard killer of women and children. I'll see you in Hell!'*

★ ★ ★

Two months had elapsed since their return to Hull, and Thomas was sitting in his office early one morning when a knock came on the door, followed by the burly figure of the captain of *The Sea Hawk*.

171

Thomas rose to his feet immediately and extended his hand in greeting. 'Good morning, captain. Pleased to see you at last. I was becoming a little worried. You are somewhat overdue, I think. What caused your delay, captain?'

He gestured to a chair, and with a look of anxiety upon his tanned features, the man sat down.

'Good morning, sir. Yes, I know I'm rather late, but with very good reason I can assure you,' and though the man answered crisply, he appeared tired and lethargic.

'It is with deep regret, sir. I have to inform you of the fact that one of my men is missing.'

Thomas looked at his visitor in feigned surprise. 'A man missing, captain. How so?'

The captain looked ill at ease. 'I don't really know sir. We were tied up in Lisbon, and one night he went ashore for a drink, and apparently never returned.'

'Do you mean he jumped ship, captain?'

'No, I don't think so sir. He was seen making his way back to the ship sometime around midnight, so I can only assume that, in a drunken state, he must have fallen in the river.'

'Who was the man?' asked Thomas, struggling to keep up this charade, for he

172

was beginning to feel sorry for the man sitting before him.

'Charlie Butlin, sir, the ship's carpenter.'

'Ah yes, I remember him. A sound tradesman. Anyway, is all this entered in the ship's log, captain?'

'Of course, sir,' he replied sharply, bristling at the thought that anyone should cast aspersions upon his seamanship.

'I had to inform the port authorities, sir, and subsequently they carried out a thorough search of all the taverns and brothels in the city, so of course that is the reason we were delayed, but all of this is entered in the ship's log, sir.'

'Very well, I can see you did everything you possibly could,' said Thomas placatingly. 'Now, are you aware of any family Charlie Butlin may have had?'

'Yes sir, a wife and daughter living in Hull. Do you wish me to inform them of their tragic loss, sir?'

'Yes please, captain, and tell his widow he was lost at sea. She will look upon his memory more kindly, than if you tell her that her late husband spent his last night on this earth out on the town getting drunk.'

The captain left, thinking what a humane, understanding person his employer was, yet relieved the interview was over.

When Thomas was alone, he sat back in his chair, just touching his granite like chin with the tips of his steepled fingers. 'Well, that takes care of you, Mr Charles Butler!' he said aloud, permitting himself a satisfied smile. 'And also, I hope, of that stupid imaginary curse, or fate or whatever it was, which seems to have been the bane of my life for so many years.'

Had Thomas Cartwright been allowed to peer into the future however, he would not have looked quite so smug, and his euphoria would have become somewhat diluted, for his fate, of which he spoke in such a derisory manner, had just one more devastating throw of the dice to make.

6

When Annie and her husband had their son christened Thomas William, no one could possibly have foreseen that some time in the future, he would work in the shipyard owned by William Earnshaw and Thomas Cartwright so, to alleviate any misunderstanding, Bull had decided his son should be known as Billy.

He and Miles had grown up together, and were closer friends than many brothers. In fact, practically inseparable for, in their free time, they went sailing, hunting, shooting and fishing together.

Then something happened which drove an ever widening wedge between the two, and though at work they still appeared compatible, and quite tolerant of each other's company, socially they went their separate ways.

It was on the occasion of Billy's twenty first birthday, and after partaking of a meal and a few drinks, the intrepid duo decided it would be a bit of a lark to visit one of the better class 'Establishments' in town.

Ironically, they chose the same 'House'

175

which Thomas had visited in his younger days, and after selecting their respective partners, Miles was taken up to the room where Maria and Thomas had first met, almost a quarter of a century previously, and where Miles had actually been conceived.

Now, whereas Billy was thrilled and overjoyed by this totally new experience of meeting with the opposite sex, and exercising his newly acquired status as an adult male, Miles was utterly disgusted, and found the whole procedure completely degrading.

For he had been brought up to treat all women with chivalry and respect, and to regard the body of a woman as something almost akin to a cathedral, where man could only enter, within the sanctity of marriage, and after a long and happy courtship, proving the love of one for the other.

Billy, however, had no such inhibitions, and continued to visit the place at every opportunity, and so the two lifelong friends inevitably drifted apart. Even when their ship docked at some foreign port, where previously they would have been content to stroll around the parks and museums, or take in the local sights of some ancient city together, now immediately they tied up, Billy was straining at the leash, to get ashore and go searching for the local girls.

He would then return in the early hours, and after waking Miles, regale him with such lurid tales of his sexual exploits that eventually Miles could take no more, and decided to ask for a transfer to another ship.

'Why, what's the trouble, Miles?' asked Thomas quizzically. 'Does Billy require a transfer too?'

'No, father. Not him!' he replied, a little too vehemently. 'And I would prefer you not to ask the reason why. It is something rather personal and private.'

Thomas surveyed his son with a feeling of pride, for he had heard of the rampant Billy's dalliance with the ladies, and he was pleased to see that Miles appeared to be intent on steering a different course, for he had wondered recently if the young roué would lead his son astray.

'All right, my boy, you shall have your transfer, and if you so wish, then I will not pry, so as far as I am concerned you may consider the matter closed.'

Miles thanked his father and returned home to Mount Pleasant for a few days shore leave, and this was the last time he and Billy would spend their leave together for, when they left, they sailed on different ships.

When Billy returned some three months

later, he was agreeably surprised to be awakened on his first morning, by a rather smart voluptuously attractive new maid.

He lay in his bed and lasciviously admired her sensual curves as she drew back the curtains, waiting until she turned, just to ascertain her face matched the rest of her. 'Good morning, gorgeous,' Billy greeted her, for when she had finally turned away from the window, he was not disappointed. 'Where have you been all my life?'

The girl flashed him a brilliant smile, showing perfect teeth. 'I am the new parlour maid, sir,' she replied, in a well modulated voice.

Billy propped himself up on one elbow. 'I see. Well I must say, you're a hell of an improvement on old Mary. Anyway, what do I call you, apart from darling?'

She blushed coquettishly, still holding the smile. 'Ivy sir, my name is Ivy.'

On a sudden impulse, Billy turned back a corner of the bed covers, and with that wicked twinkle in his eye which so many others before Ivy had found irresistible, he said. 'Care to hop in Ivy, and cling to me for a while?'

The blush remained the same pale pink, and with perfect poise she replied. 'I would love to, sir, but I am afraid it is impossible during the morning.'

She turned to go, and Billy who, for once in his chequered career, was momentarily speechless and didn't manage to find his voice until she reached the door, called to her. 'How about tonight, then?'

Ivy stayed her hand as she was on the point of opening the door, and turned towards him, and with no smile this time, but a dreamy far away look in her eyes. 'Possibly,' she murmured, and was gone.

Billy moped around the house all morning, and in the afternoon rode into town, but he had returned by eight o'clock that evening.

'My word, you are home early,' Annie greeted him, as she met him in the hall, hoping fervently her son had mended his ways. 'Especially considering this is your first night ashore for some time.'

'Yes, I know, mother. You would never believe it, but all my friends seemed like young kids tonight. Do you think I might be growing up, mother?'

Annie smiled fondly upon her only son. 'I certainly hope so, Billy. You have no idea how much your father and I worry about you, particularly when you persist in staying out late at night.'

Billy mentally hugged himself with anticipation. By, if only she knew why

I'm home early tonight, he thought, and then wondered bleakly, how the devil he was going to while away the next two or three hours.

Just before midnight, when everyone was asleep and the house was quiet, and Billy was preparing to go to Ivy's room, his bedroom door opened, then closed very softly, and a slim ghostly figure slipped in, and in the twinkling of an eye, Ivy was in his arms.

That night, and each succeeding night for as long as Billy's leave lasted, the two lovers assuaged their mutual sexual lust.

'Don't you ever worry about becoming pregnant, Ivy?' asked Billy, after one particularly enchanting union.

'Of course not, don't be silly, and anyway if I do you will stand by me, and then one day I shall be mistress of all this,' she replied, spreading her naked arms in an expansive gesture.

Billy, however, was far too immersed in her nubile breasts to take any notice of what she was saying, and so the only warning he ever received completely passed him by.

A big, rough-looking fellow, obviously a farmer, who went by the name of Luke Carlton, was standing at a bar in town having a drink when by pure chance he overheard this well dressed, good-looking

180

brash young man boasting to his friends of his many conquests with the opposite sex.

Now Luke was staring bankruptcy in the face, for his farm had been losing money over the last couple of years. In fact, in desperation, he had visited both Beverly and York races, hoping for a substantial win, but unfortunately his luck at picking winners had proved no better than his luck with the farm.

As he stood there and listened to this boastful young whippersnapper, Luke began to have an idea, which under normal circumstances, he would never have considered, but these were desperate times, and he thought at last he may be able to see light at the end of the tunnel.

Later that day Luke made discreet enquiries about that certain young man. Who he was, where he worked, where he lived, and the ultimate outcome of these enquiries, were far more revealing and much more satisfying than he had ever dared hope. The end result of Luke's questioning and probing, was his daughter Ivy applying for the position of housemaid at Mount Pleasant.

Prior to leaving home to take up her new post, Ivy had received strict instructions from her father on how to conduct herself when the young master arrived home on leave.

However, much of this fell on deaf ears, for the girl was far more experienced than either of her parents ever suspected.

Billy was actually pleased when his leave expired, for he was thankfully looking forward to some respite from Ivy's insatiable sexual appetite.

He had been at sea approximately two months, while in the meantime Miles had returned to Mount Pleasant.

He was sitting in the drawing room with his mother and father, when Milton entered. 'Excuse me, sir,' said the butler, addressing Thomas. 'There is a rough-looking individual at the front entrance, wishes to speak to you.'

'Very well, thank you, Milton,' replied Thomas, as he stood up and followed Milton out into the hall. Luke Carlton was more than slightly taken aback when he saw the size of the man he had come to threaten.

'Does your son live here with you?' he blustered.

'Yes, he does,' replied Thomas quietly. 'Though what business that is of yours, I cannot imagine.'

'Oh, you cannot?' mimicked the farmer. 'Well please allow me to tell you, mister. My Ivy works here in this house, and your randy son has got her pregnant!'

He never saw Thomas move, but suddenly the heavily built farmer found himself slammed against the wall, with an arm which felt like an iron band across his throat, and as he stared into his assailant's eyes, he saw death lurking there.

'*What did you say?*' The voice was reminiscent of a silken thread being drawn very slowly across the lips, and Luke Carlton shivered involuntarily.

'I said your son has made my Ivy pregnant,' he stammered, as he felt the cold sweat begin to trickle down his back.

'Is there anything I can do, sir?' Milton, having heard the noise outside, had decided to investigate.

'Yes Milton,' replied Thomas calmly, as he removed his arm. 'You may ask my son to come out here, and also send Ivy.'

Thomas walked down the steps to the drive, and Luke followed him. A moment later Miles appeared with Ivy by his side. Ivy's hand flew to her mouth when she saw her father.

'Go on lass, tell him,' he shouted, his courage returning now he was out of the reach of Thomas.

'Tell him what father?' mumbled the frightened girl

'What you told me. That his randy son

made you pregnant!' he roared.

'But I didn't,' protested Miles vehemently. 'I only returned home last night, after two months at sea.'

'Don't you deny it, you young b . . . '

His daughter was screaming at him. 'It wasn't him father, it was the other one!'

Her father appeared bemused. Yet when he looked at Miles, he could see this was not the young man he had heard in the bar that day.

'Other one. Do you have two sons?' he asked, addressing Thomas.

'No, only this one,' he replied, with a smile which irritated the farmer even more.

'Are you the owner of this estate?' Luke asked, finding it difficult to hold his temper in check.

'Yes, I am,' answered Thomas, smiling more broadly than ever, and deriving a certain sadistic enjoyment from the obvious frustration of his most unattractive visitor.

Suddenly the farmer wheeled around and faced his daughter. 'You stupid little whore!' he shouted. 'I told you to go after the son of the house,' accompanying this tirade with a heavy flat handed blow to the poor girl's cheek, sending her crashing to the ground.

In almost the same instant, Luke Carlton hit the gravelled drive beside his daughter.

'Who the hell are you?' he spluttered, through a bloodied mouth and swiftly swelling lips, as he lay there, looking up at the mountain of a man standing over him.

'I, my friend am Billy's father. I'm the one you should be talking to. Also, we are not in the habit of hitting our women, especially when they are pregnant,' snarled Bull contemptuously, as he bent and gently helped the sobbing girl to her feet.

'Now, if you want to hit somebody, have a go at me, otherwise climb on your horse and ride out of here, before I tear your arms off.'

As he looked up at the granite faced menacing figure towering above him, Luke never doubted for a second that the man was quite capable of carrying out his threat and, deciding it was much better to be a live whole coward, than a maimed armless hero, he hurriedly scrambled to his feet and, reaching for his horse, which was grazing quietly nearby, pulled himself up into the saddle. Amid derisive laughter from those whom he had set out to threaten, and then to fleece, and a shout of, 'See you in church!' from Bull, he quickly disappeared down the drive.

As they all turned to go into the house, Ivy approached Bull. 'Excuse me, Mr Hyde,' she said softly. 'Why did you tell my father you would see him in church?'

Bull looked at the girl appraisingly. 'Because, my dear Ivy, I will. If, as you say, that lad of mine has got you in trouble, then he will marry you. Make no mistake about that.'

Even though the girl nursed her bruised and swollen cheek, her eyes shone with happiness. 'Oh! Thank you, Mr Hyde. But this wasn't all Billy's fault you know. As my father said, he did send me to work here to try and seduce the son of the house. Though I'm pleased I made a mistake and went to Billy's room instead,' she added with a smile.

Bull made no reply, for he was too full of admiration, and too surprised by the girl's open honesty, and the frank admission of her own guilt. As no one spoke, Ivy continued. 'My father isn't so bad, Mr Hyde. His bark is far worse than his bite. That is the first time he has ever hit me, and I know he is in terrible financial trouble regarding the farm. You see, he has worked so hard to make a go of it, and now he is scared of losing everything.'

Thomas stepped forward. 'Where is your father's farm, Ivy?' he asked, touched by the girl's pleading defence of the father, who only moments earlier had knocked her to the ground.

A week later, Thomas turned off the Beverly road, through an open gateway bearing a crudely painted sign 'Carlton's Farm,' nailed to one of the rotting gateposts.

He followed what was nothing more than a deeply rutted farm track, passing on either side, fields of proudly standing golden corn. He reined in his horse, and bending low in the saddle snapped off an ear from its strong stalk, and after rubbing it between the palms of his hands, and then blowing away the chaff, he tested a couple of grains with his teeth.

Continuing down the track, he rounded a bend and suddenly there in front of him stood a squat farmhouse, with a good sized stockyard and the farm buildings surrounding it.

There was an air of, not poverty, but dilapidation about the place. The house needed repainting and the roofs of some of the outbuildings, could do with a lick of tar.

Luke Carlton appeared in the doorway of his kitchen. 'What do you want?' he greeted sullenly. 'Have you come to gloat?'

Thomas slid easily from the saddle. He answered the surly farmer's questions with two of his own. 'What are you doing in the house at this time of day, man? Why aren't you out there cutting that corn? It is in perfect condition, and prime for cutting now, especially on a day such as this.'

The farmer emitted a short embarrassed laugh. 'Tell me something I don't already know.'

They were closer now, and Luke Carlton looked keenly at his visitor. He knew he had to tell somebody, and this chap appeared trustworthy enough, so throwing caution to the winds he decided to take the plunge. 'Just tie your horse to that post, and come for a walk,' he said quietly.

Intrigued, Thomas did as he was bid, and together they walked around the back of the house, skirting a meadow of tall waving grass, fanned by a gentle summer breeze, and after a short silence, the farmer summoned up sufficient courage to pour out his troubles.

'Look, I'm not pleading poverty, mister, but I'm at my wit's end. I know that corn is ripe and ready for harvesting, I know this field is waiting to be scythed and turned into hay, but you see I just can't afford the labour. The bank is about to foreclose on me, and I have nothing more to sell to pay the men's wages. There, I've told you now. I've never breathed a word of this to anybody, and it hurts like hell telling you. I just had to tell somebody,' he finished lamely.

Thomas looked at the man with his piercing blue eyes, and though Luke had the uneasy feeling his brain was being taken apart, he never lowered his own.

At length, Thomas lifted his head and gazed around him at this typical English scene, and he hated the thought of what might happen to this highly productive land, and this obviously hard working farmer, if the 'townies' from the bank, and others of similar ilk, were to get their money grabbing hands on it.

On a sudden impulse, he turned to his companion and held out his hand. 'Right, Luke Carlton. Though we first met in rather unfortunate circumstances, things can only get better. Make sure you are up and about by dawn tomorrow, and I will have twenty men and possibly the same number of women here, to help you bring your harvest home.'

Luke Carlton, who had only met his benefactor once before, willingly accepted the hand offered to him, and shook it warmly. 'But what about paying the wages?' he protested.

Thomas smiled. 'Let me take care of that,

Luke, then you can pay me after you have sold your corn.'

It would have been impossible to have found a tougher type of man than Luke Carlton, hardened as he was, living through many winters on his lonely farm, often isolated from the outside world by huge snowdrifts. Yet, as this visitor rode away, a tear trickled unashamedly down his leathery weather beaten cheek, and he didn't even bother to brush it away.

The day her father had visited Mount Pleasant, Ivy had unwittingly and quite innocently become the instrument that would create a bond of friendship between the Cartwrights and the Carltons, which would outlast the lives of these two men, and continue to sustain their families well into the next century, and for many generations to come.

Billy had finally arrived home from his latest voyage, and after a terrible row with his parents, because of Ivy's condition, for he was not enthralled by the thought of being tied down to a wife and a baby. He went out for a long walk alone.

No one ever discovered what happened to Billy on that particular walk but, when he returned, apparently he had been doing an awful lot of thinking, for now he was a changed man, and much more than that, he seemed quite taken with the idea of becoming a father!

After their marriage, he and Ivy moved into a small house near the centre of town, and Thomas arranged Billy's sailings, so he was home for his wife's confinement. Billy was very proud of being the father of a beautiful baby girl, and now, when he visited some foreign port, his usual nightly romantic excursions, were replaced by investigating around local shops during the afternoons, searching for some exotic bargain priced presents, to take home for his wife and child.

To everyone's surprise and delight, Ivy became the perfect mother and homemaker, blissfully happy with her husband and their new baby. However, what intrigued his parents more than anything else, and particularly Miles, was the way Billy had so enthusiastically settled down to a life of marital domesticity.

Fourteen months after their first child was born, Ivy gave birth to a son, and this event resulted in Billy and Miles getting very drunk that night, to celebrate what Billy called, 'his coming of age,' and 'proving he was a man.'

For, since his marriage, and total abstinence

from his usual sexual flings of the past, he and Miles had resumed their old friendship, and Miles would often call to see Ivy and the children on his way home from the yard, particularly if Billy was away at sea.

On one such occasion during the summer of that year, Miles knocked upon Ivy's door and walked in, to be greeted by a stalwart youth of about the same age as himself.

'Good evening,' said the stranger cordially, extending his hand. 'You must be Billy.'

Miles accepted the proffered hand. 'No,' he replied with a smile. 'I am Miles Cartwright.'

The young man looked confused, but fortunately at that moment Ivy appeared in the hallway. 'Oh Miles, I am pleased you have called. I see you have already met my brother. Matthew this is . . . '

'I know, he has just introduced himself. Honestly, I thought he was your husband,' he replied, cutting his sister off in mid-sentence. 'Come along through, Miles, and I will introduce you to my wife. I'm sorry for jumping to the wrong conclusion.'

Miles followed them into the room, and a rather short buxom young lady rose from her chair to meet them.

'Hazel, this is Mr Miles Cartwright,' said Matthew. When the introductions were over, Miles turned to Ivy.

'I had no idea you had a brother Ivy — '
he began, but again Matthew interrupted.
He seemed to have a habit of speaking out
of turn.

'No, of course you hadn't. Ivy would never
tell anybody, because she wasn't very proud
of me like. You see, Miles, nearly three
years ago I left home and went down
south to seek my fortune. The farm wasn't
doing very well, and I was always rowing
with our dad, so one day I just up and
left. Anyway I got a job on this farm
outside London, and to cut a long story
short, I seduced Hazel, who happened to
be the farmer's daughter, then when her
condition showed like, her old man threw
me out, and she told him that if I went
she was leaving too, so now you know why
we're here.'

'Have you been to see your father yet,
Matthew?' asked Miles, attempting to rescue
his hat from the little girl's sticky fingers, for
both Ivy's children were in the room.

'Yes, I have made it up with him and
ma, and we are going to live out there on
the farm.' Suddenly he smote his thigh.
'Cartwright! Of course. You must be the
son of Thomas Cartwright. My father seems
to think he is some kind of God, for he
spoke of nothing else last night, telling me

how your father saved our farm from certain bankruptcy.

'Apparently, a couple of years ago he sent about three dozen men and women to help with the harvest. He came himself and brought Billy's dad with him, and according to what my old man said, them two worked flat out all day, doing twice as much work as anybody else like. He'd never seen men work so hard, and by tea time all the corn was cut, gathered into sheaves and stooked. Thank him very much from me Miles, and please tell him I am looking forward to making his acquaintance.'

Miles smiled to himself, for such stories of his father's generosity were legion, throughout the county. He eased a finger around his collar, as a feeling of claustrophobia swept over him, and he realised he would have to get out of this small room, crowded as it was with four adults and two noisy children. So, as unhurried and as courteous as possible, Miles bade them farewell.

As the years slipped by, Miles spent more of his time in the office, and Thomas gradually allowed the reins of power to be passed to his son, who some years previously had studied accountancy, and now proved himself to be a formidable businessman, and well able to take control of the helm, if and when his father decided to retire.

Sometimes, Thomas and Maria would look at their son, and wonder if he would ever marry and present them with their first grandchild.

Thomas mentioned this matter after supper one evening. 'Do you ever have any lady friends, Miles?' he asked abruptly.

Maria looked shocked. 'Darling, you could have been a little more diplomatic,' she murmured.

Miles laughed. 'Mother, have you ever known father to be diplomatic about anything?' Then turning to Thomas. 'No father, I haven't, nor can I visualise one in the foreseeable future. However, I am far too busy at the moment even to contemplate being tied to some woman's apron strings.'

He laughed again when he saw the look on his father's face. 'Father, please do not look so disappointed. Obviously I am not the marrying kind. Anyway, what brought this on?'

Thomas coughed. 'Well your mother and I were discussing various family matters, and we realised that you will be thirty years old next week, and we haven't been blessed with a grandchild, and so far as I can see, never will be.'

'You could be right father, for I have

never yet seen the woman with whom I could spend the rest of my life, except of course you mama.

'Goodnight you two, I'm off to bed, to dream about that angel wife, who is waiting out there somewhere just for me and, father, please don't worry about the old lineage running out. Not yet for a while anyway,' he chuckled as he closed the door.

However, the happy go lucky bachelor days of Miles Cartwright were to end much sooner than he or his parents could ever have anticipated. For it was a bizarre set of circumstances indeed which culminated in the meeting of his first, last and only love of his life.

7

The youngest of Billy and Ivy's two children had reached the age of seven, when in the early summer of that year, Ivy fell very ill, with what the doctor had diagnosed as a summer cold.

He had quickly changed his opinion however, on his second visit, when he could find no improvement in her condition. Fortunately Billy was at home on shore leave, and the doctor informed him in no uncertain terms, that it was absolutely essential he removed his wife from her present environment, for the everyday stench from the surrounding factories was affecting her lungs, and he stated categorically that an extended holiday by the sea, would be her only hope.

Billy was at his wit's end, as he couldn't possibly afford to send Ivy to the coast for a few days, never mind a long holiday and in desperation he turned to his old friend.

Miles was terribly upset and most concerned when he heard of Ivy's illness. However after a few moments thought, he arrived at the perfect solution. 'Listen Billy. We have a house standing empty at Scarborough. I will explain everything to father, and in the morning I will call at your house with a coach, to collect you and your family.'

'But I don't have any spare money to pay you for the house,' wailed Billy.

Miles placed his arm around Billy's shoulders. 'Look old chap, you are my friend, so please do not even think of offering me any money. As I say, the house is empty anyway, so I shall drive the coach tomorrow, and probably stay a few days to help you settle in, for I could do with a holiday myself.'

Tears were streaming unchecked down Billy's cheeks, as he gripped the hand of his benefactor. 'Thank you Miles,' he whispered brokenly. 'I shall never forget this,' and a rather embarrassed Miles bade him a hasty farewell.

Thomas had agreed immediately with his son's proposal, and had even suggested Miles should stay for the week, if he so wished.

The day they arrived was a Saturday, and the following morning, Miles as always, went to church. However, the church he normally attended whilst in Scarborough, was closed for repairs, and by the time he had found an alternative one the service had already started, so he had to sit in a pew right at the back, for the church was almost full.

When he eventually lifted his head, the first hymn was over and the congregation were seated. It was at that moment that Miles caught his breath. For sitting immediately in front of him, was a girl with the most beautiful head of chestnut coloured hair he had ever seen, and though she wore a hat, this only served to accentuate the thick rich natural waves, falling tumultuously to her shoulders.

Miles sat rooted to the spot, thinking he must be having an hallucination, for he was sure he had seen this girl before, many years ago when he was a child, but that was impossible, for she still appeared so young.

Now the congregation was standing again, and they were singing 'Rock of Ages,' his Great Aunt Lottie's favourite hymn, and suddenly, through the mists of time. He remembered.

That was it! This girl standing so proud and erect in the next pew, reminded him of his Great Aunt. She had the same tall slim figure and the same glorious hair, though as he looked more closely, he could see this girl's hair was several shades darker, almost like burnished copper.

Miles was determined that after the service he would somehow have to introduce himself to her, though he had not the remotest idea how he could possibly accomplish that feat, and still be regarded as a gentleman.

The parson seemed to drone on endlessly over his sermon, and by the time the final 'Amen' was sung, Miles was almost a nervous wreck. However, the Gods smiled down upon him that day for, as he walked out of the church, immediately behind the girl, a sudden heaven sent gust of wind whipped the wide brimmed hat off the head of her older companion, who was walking by her side.

Miles saw his opportunity, and like a greyhound springing from the trap, he shot across the churchyard in hot pursuit of the recalcitrant head piece, as it bowled capriciously among the sun-dappled graves, finally coming to rest at the base of a headstone.

He retrieved the flimsy piece of material with a muttered 'Bless you,' and returned triumphantly to the waiting women, where he even amazed himself. Because, for the last eight years he had avoided the opposite sex like the plague, but now, with an exaggerated flourish and his most disarming smile, he handed his prize to the bare headed, highly embarrassed lady, with the words. 'Miles Cartwright, at your service madam.'

The woman returned his smile and held

out her gloved hands, one to receive her hat, the other to shake that of Miles. 'Thank you very much, kind sir,' she replied. 'Please allow me to introduce my daughter, Ruth.'

With admirable nonchalance, considering the way his heart was pounding, Miles shifted his attention to the lovely creature standing by her mother's side. He stifled a gasp. For she was far more beautiful than he had ever dared hope. Her eyes were as green as some of the seas he had traversed on his many voyages and when she blinked, as she did at that moment against the bright sunlight, her long lashes came down like a golden curtain.

He took her small dainty hand in his large masculine one, and as their eyes locked, though her hand was gloved, he experienced a highly pleasurable tingling sensation ricochet through his body. 'Extremely pleased to make your acquaintance, Miss Ruth,' he somehow managed to say.

Reluctantly he had to release the hand of this lovely girl, for her mother was speaking again, and bringing all his concentration to bear, for she seemed to be speaking from a great distance, he turned his attention to what the older woman was saying.

'Did you say your name is Miles Cartwright?' she asked, as causally as if she was enquiring what time the tide changed, and when he replied in the affirmative, she continued in the same light hearted vein. 'Are you a member of the Cartwright shipbuilding family?'

Miles smiled to himself. He had been asked this same question countless times before by other aspiring females. This time however, he didn't seem to mind. In fact he felt proud and inordinately pleased to be able to answer. 'Yes, my father, Thomas Cartwright, is the owner.'

They were walking towards the lychgate now, and the woman had manoeuvred the young couple so that Miles was between her and her daughter.

When Lucy had learned of her beloved Charlie's disappearance and reported death at sea, her whole world had crumbled, but then her late husband's solicitor had called to inform her of the thousands Charlie had bequeathed to her in his will. Of course, all this money came as a complete surprise to her and at the time seemed like a fortune, which helped to bring solace to her troubled spirit, and also provided a cushion on which she could rebuild her shattered life.

However, one year later, the solicitor had called again, this time requiring her signature for the sale of the five hundred acres of land, old Sam had left Charlie in Australia.

Apparently Sydney was expanding dramatically, and this particular tract of land was prime building land and ripe for development, which a company wished to purchase for the mind blowing sum of *One Hundred and Fifty Thousand Pounds!*

Immediately Lucy had received the money, she had sold her inn, and moved out to a large detached house standing in approximately ten acres of grounds in the country. She was a very wealthy widow now, and had naturally become an obvious target for every predatory middle aged bachelor and widower in the county.

However, showing great skill and quite often more than a little duplicity, she had managed to fend off all comers, and even now had still succeeded in maintaining her independence.

Recently however, a different age group had tried to worm their way into Lucy's attractive, though very private lifestyle. For with her daughter growing into such a lovely, desirable young lady, and her mother's wealth adding a further attraction, all the local young Lotharios had called seeking her hand, but to no avail. Her mother, having had so much practice and, over the years, becoming wise to the ways of men, had no difficulty in sorting the wheat from the chaff, and having decided they were all chaff anyway, had sent each and every one away from her domain with a flea in his ear.

For Lucy was determined, that if and when her daughter married, it would have to be to someone of impeccable character and family background. Also someone who could at least match her own wealth, for she would never allow her money to be squandered in later years by a hard drinking, gambling dissolute son-in-law.

Lucy's mind was ticking over as smoothly as the gold hunter in Miles's waistcoat pocket and, as she stole a sidelong glance at the young man strolling so easily and with such style, between herself and her elegantly dressed daughter, she silently thanked God she had allowed Ruth to persuade her to come to church that morning, for Lucy could always recognise real class when she saw it.

She also admired his height and breadth of shoulders and, though she had to admit he must be several years older than her daughter, she didn't mind, for that would mean he had outgrown the dreams and fantasies of youth, and would prove to be exactly as he appeared, handsome, solid, dependable and *rich!*

They had reached the lychgate and Lucy was jolted out of her mercenary reverie, by the hand of Miles holding her arm and gently guiding her down the steps and onto the footpath, and Lucy smiled as she thought, What a delicious sensation, to have a real gentleman touch her, and be sufficiently concerned to aid her progress, if only for a moment.

Miles moved ahead, turned and faced them. 'Now, where do you live, ma'am?'

Lucy smiled. 'Lucy. Miles, please call me Lucy,' she said, in an endearingly familiar way. 'And if you really wish to know, our name is Myers.'

'Very well, Ruth and Lucy Myers. Where in Scarborough do you live?' he enquired, matching Lucy's smile but, taking great care, he included Ruth.

They both laughed aloud at his question. 'We do not live in Scarborough. We are simply staying here for a short holiday. Actually we live just outside Hull,' replied Lucy.

Miles acknowledged the humour of his question, and joined in their laughter. 'Hull, you say? Well, that of course makes everything simple, doesn't it?'

'How do you mean, simple?' asked the lovely Ruth, in such a shy innocent way, totally devoid of any affectation, which only served to increase the determination of Miles to see more of this wonderful girl.

'What I mean, my dear, is that if you live in Hull, I shall have the opportunity to visit you quite often,' then turning quickly to Lucy. 'That is, of course, with the kind permission of your mama.'

Lucy was thrilled that such a man, of the calibre and family background as Miles Cartwright, should wish to call upon her daughter. She had seen the obvious adoration in his eyes when he looked at Ruth, but had never dared hope he would wish to prolong their short acquaintance beyond this holiday.

'Of course you may visit us Miles. You must come to dinner one evening, immediately we return home. Now, where are you staying in Scarborough?'

'My father bought a house several years ago, overlooking the Spa, and I'm staying there with a friend and his family,' replied Miles, highly gratified with Lucy's invitation.

'Oh! How convenient,' murmured Ruth. 'We are on the same road, in a small private hotel.'

When Miles returned to the house late that evening, he was confronted by Billy. 'Where have you been all day and half the night?' he demanded belligerently.

Miles only smiled, and replied happily.

'Oh, just out. You know, here and there, though it was rather a long sermon.'

Billy however, refused to be put off as easily as that. 'Long sermon my eye. You went to church this morning. And here and there, that's no sort of an answer,' he persisted. 'No, according to the way you look my friend, I would say you have met a girl. Am I right?'

Miles was quick to realise it would be impossible to deceive Billy for long and, anyway, he was bursting to confide in someone, and who better than his oldest friend.

'Your perception old chap, is only exceeded by the size of your head. I never realised my feelings were so obvious, but yes, you are quite right, I have met a girl. A stunning, beautiful girl, and if she will have me, one day I intend to make her my wife!'

Billy collapsed in the nearest chair, his face a picture of incredulity. 'But Miles,' he spluttered. 'You haven't been with a girl for years. You're out of touch. You only met her today. I mean, you don't know anything about her, not really, or her family.'

Miles interrupted him. 'Billy, I have met her and her mother, and for the very first time in my life I am in love.' He then gave his friend a resume of what had transpired that memorable day, and when he had finished, all Billy could say was. 'Well I've heard of love at first sight, but this is barmy.'

Miles laughed aloud at his friend's remark. 'I know, but isn't it wonderful?' he replied happily.

However, Billy was to change his attitude the following morning, when Miles brought Ruth and her mother to see Ivy and the children.

After the introductions had been made, the two friends went for a walk and a breath of air in the garden, leaving Ruth and Lucy in rapturous delight over the children. Immediately they were out of sight from the open French windows, Miles turned to his companion. 'Well. What do you think? Isn't she just as beautiful as I said?'

'Beautiful!' ejaculated Billy enthusiastically. 'How the devil do you get anyone so adorable to even look twice at such a miserable old codger as you?' he asked facetiously.

'I really don't know,' laughingly replied Miles. 'But I do know I fully intend to do my very best to make her keep looking.'

'You don't think her mother is trying a little match making because of your money, do you?' asked Billy, on a more serious note.

Miles smiled, a quite serene kind of smile, like a man who, for the first time in his life had found the road to true happiness. 'No, my friend. I do not think that for one moment. You see, the private hotel they are staying in just down the road, her mother actually owns. Apparently, when Ruth's father died, he left a small fortune, and his widow has been worried sick over the chance that her daughter might fall in love with some man who only wanted her because of their money.

'Her mother seems very sensible where money is concerned, and that small hotel is just one of her several investments. So you see, I believe for the first time in my life, I have found a young lady who is actually interested in me, and not solely because of who I am, or what I own.'

'Ah well,' sighed Billy. 'As my old granddad used to say. Apples always fall where there's orchards.'

So, the long halcyon days of that unforgettable summer's vacation passed swiftly by and the two lovers, bathed, serenely happy, in the first flush of the springtime of their new found love.

None knew better than Miles, that 'Time and Tide wait for no man' and, far too quickly, the weekend was upon them. He and Ruth were strolling hand in hand along the promenade, for once unchaperoned by the over indulgent Lucy, completely oblivious of the holiday crowds enjoying the evening sunshine. For Miles was leaving in the morning and this would be their last few moments together, until she and her mother returned to Hull.

'When may I see you again?' he asked abruptly.

She turned to him, her lovely eyes clouded with sadness. 'I really don't know my dearest,' she answered softly. 'You see everything depends on mama, but I promise you, I will do all I can to persuade her to cut this holiday short.'

He squeezed her hand. 'If there were not so many people watching, I would kiss you, Ruth Myers,' said Miles, devouring her youthful beauty, as he looked down at her with adoration in his eyes. Ruth reciprocated his look, and whispered almost bashfully. 'I do love you so, Miles. Somehow, I will let you know immediately we return, and then you must come and see me.'

Unknown to either of them however, Lucy had already arranged to return home with her daughter, leaving Scarborough an hour after Miles. For, as she had watched the relationship develop during the past week between Ruth and this man, she had no intention of allowing such a prodigiously eligible bachelor as Miles Cartwright, slip through her fingers.

When they returned to the hotel later that evening, Lucy had prepared supper for them and, soon after the meal, Ruth asked to be excused for a moment. Two minutes later she came dashing downstairs. 'Mama, why have you started packing our trunks?' she cried excitedly.

Lucy looked upon her daughter lovingly, and with a knowing smile, quietly replied. 'Because my dear, I think we have had enough of Scarborough for this year, and I fully intended leaving tomorrow, but of course if you wish to stay for a further week, I can quite easily unpack.'

'Oh no, mama. It would be a terrible shame to cause you all that trouble unnecessarily. What time are we leaving in the morning?'

'I have ordered a coach for ten o'clock.'

Ruth turned ecstatically to Miles. 'Darling, did you hear what mama said? We are going home tomorrow!'

'Yes, my dear, I heard. I do not wish to appear over presumptuous Lucy, but I shall be driving an empty coach to Hull tomorrow, and wondered if perhaps yourself and your daughter would care to accompany me?'

The excited anticipation with which Miles asked, was not lost on Lucy, yet she did not wish to appear too eager to accept his courteous offer, though it fitted in so beautifully with her own plans for Ruth.

'Thank you, Miles. That would be wonderful, and is most gracious of you, but surely you will have a full load with your friends and their children, and anyway I have ordered the coach now.'

He saw the eager look of happiness die in Ruth's lovely eyes, and knew he somehow had to convince her mother to travel with him.

Miles gave that brilliant smile Ruth so loved to see, which also caused him to appear much younger. 'I think we may be able to surmount those two problems, ladies. In the first instance, Ivy has made such a remarkable recovery whilst enjoying the fresh sea air and sunshine during the past week, I have decided to extend Billy's shore leave for a further week, so if you don't come with me, I shall be travelling alone. In the second instance, I will cancel your coach first thing in the morning Lucy, but in order to save the driver any loss of earnings, I will engage him to drive my coach.'

'Yes, Miles. That all sounds very well, but how will the driver be able to return to Scarborough?' asked Lucy.

Ruth watched this wonderful man with bated breath, knowing instinctively that he would provide an answer.

'Quite easily,' replied Miles, now confident he would be successful, in his bid to escort Lucy and her lovely daughter back to their home. 'I shall simply instruct him to tie another horse to the rear of the coach, and then he can ride him when he returns.'

Lucy smiled. Inwardly she was elated by the outcome of this short holiday, and was secretly formulating great plans for her daughter's future, when Ruth broke in upon her thoughts.

'Please say you agree, mama,' she pleaded. 'I am sure it would be rather silly to drive two coaches all that way, just to carry three people.'

'Yes, my dear, of course I agree. Thank you very much for the offer Miles, I . . . ' However, the end of her remark was lost amidst the folds of her daughter's luxuriant hair, as Ruth embraced her mother, almost smothering her in the process.

* * *

'I have always admired this house,' said Miles, as they passed through the gateway and continued along a drive flanked on either side by majestic elms, almost hiding the many gabled, large, red brick house from the view of anyone walking or riding along the road.

'Why, do you ride past very often?' asked Lucy, feigning only a mild interest, yet burning with curiosity as to why Miles Cartwright should pass by the entrance to her drive.

He laughed. 'Only twice a day,' he replied.

'Twice a day!' echoed Ruth, her eyes shining. 'How wonderful. Do you mean every day?'

'Yes, my dear, I mean every day. You see, I live with my parents at Mount Pleasant. It is just a small place overlooking the Humber, and I ride by each day to the shipyard.'

'Small place, indeed,' cried Lucy. 'We have seen your Mount Pleasant, well the entrance anyway, when we have been out in the trap. It is a huge estate. The drive is so long and lined with trees, we couldn't even see the house. Well fancy that, I have often wondered who lived there, and now I know.'

After digesting this snippet of information, Lucy became more determined than ever to give this very eligible young man every encouragement she deemed necessary to bring his short acquaintance with her daughter to a fruitful and admirable conclusion.

As the coach came to a halt in front of the stone pillared entrance, Miles jumped down and helped Lucy and her daughter alight. Then, after paying and dismissing the driver, he proceeded to carry their luggage into the house.

'Oh Miles,' purred Lucy, as she studied how easily he carried the heavy trunk. 'It is so wonderful to have a real man about the place.'

Miles smiled his appreciation, as he staggered past her and on up the steps.

An elderly couple lived in the rear of the house. The man tending the large garden, while his wife cleaned and cooked for Lucy and her daughter.

'My goodness ma'am, we never expected you to come home today,' wailed the housekeeper, as she met them in the hall. 'I don't have any tea ready for you, but it won't take long if I pop the kettle on now.'

'Thank you, Hannah, that will be lovely,' replied Lucy graciously. Then, turning to Miles. 'You will stay and have some tea, won't you Miles? It is the least I can offer you by way of appreciation for bringing us home.'

'No, thank you, Lucy. I still have to return

the coach and horses to the yard. However, I would love to call and have supper on my way home, if I may,' he added quickly, as he saw the look of disappointment shadow her daughter's eyes.

'Oh yes please, Miles,' cried Ruth. 'That will be all right, won't it, mama?'

As the two returned to the house, after waving goodbye to Miles, Ruth turned to her mother. 'Mama, isn't he just delicious? whatever have I done to deserve such a wonderful man?'

Lucy smiled. 'I have no idea, but whatever it was you had better continue in the same vein, for if you allow Miles Cartwright to slip through your fingers, I shall never forgive you.'

The lamp lit windows of Mount Pleasant emitted a welcoming glow, as Miles rode up the darkened drive later that night, and an owl hooted in a nearby tree as he clattered into the cobbled courtyard, and handed the reins of his mount to a weary-looking groomsman.

His parents were in the drawing room. Apparently, they had heard his approach on the gravelled drive, and had set aside their books while they waited for him to enter the room.

Immediately the door opened, Maria

rushed to his side. 'Oh! Miles, wherever have you been until now?' she cried, as she lovingly embraced her son, kissing him upon the cheek. 'It is so unlike you to be late. Your father and I have been worried sick, afraid something must have happened to you on the road from Scarborough.'

'Hello, mother, father,' he replied, smiling as he gently released himself from Maria's embrace. 'No, nothing happened to me on the road. I'm sorry if you have been unduly worried, and before you ask, yes, I have had a most marvellous week.'

'I will ring for some supper dear. You must be famished after travelling all that way,' said Maria, moving towards the bell rope.

'No, thank you, mother. That will not be necessary, I have already eaten,' he replied. Then, trying to steer the conversation away from himself, and any further questioning, he turned to Thomas.

'Ivy has made such a wonderful recovery, father I have given Billy permission to stay on for a further week. I hope you don't mind. I'm sure we can rearrange his sailing on another ship.'

'Of course, I don't mind son. Billy's no use to us if he is going to be fretting about his wife all the time he's at sea. Anyway, I'm pleased to hear Ivy is improving, evidently the doctor was correct when he said all she needed was a change of air. That reminds me, is your cottage still empty Maria?'

'Yes dear. Why?' asked Maria, wondering what mad suggestion this wonderful, yet so unpredictable man of hers was going to come up with now.

'Well, I was thinking that when Billy, his wife and children return from Scarborough, perhaps you would consider allowing them to rent your cottage.'

'I say father. That is a terrific idea. Please say you agree mother. If you had seen how pale and wan Ivy was before she left Hull, and could see the difference in her today, I am sure you would not hesitate.'

'Very well, if you two think that is the proper course to take, and is so important for the continued good health of Ivy, then so be it.'

'Thank you, both of you. I can't wait to tell Billy, for I know how much he will appreciate this gesture,' said Miles, in the middle of a protracted yawn. 'I'm afraid I shall have to go to bed. This seems to have been a very long day.'

He moved toward his mother to kiss her goodnight, but she placed her hand upon his arm and stopped him, for Maria, with her uncanny intuitive powers of detecting the slightest change in anyone's demeanour, particularly those close to her, had sensed something different about Miles, immediately he had entered the room.

Normally she could read her son like a book, but not this evening, and she suspected him of hiding something. 'Just one moment dear, before you go,' said his mother, smiling sweetly. 'You said you had eaten earlier. Do you mind telling us where?'

Miles knew from past experience, he would not be able to fool his mother for long, and was well prepared for her expected question. 'Not at all mother,' he replied nonchalantly. 'I met some people in Scarborough and, during the week, discovered they lived in Hull and were travelling home today, so quite naturally I offered to bring them home in my otherwise empty coach. Well they were so grateful that, after I had returned the coach and horses to the yard, they invited me to call in and have supper. That is all mother, as simple as that.' He bent and kissed her. 'Goodnight you two, and sleep well,' and he was gone.

Thomas looked up and saw Maria's puckered brow. 'What's wrong my dear. You look worried. Is it Ivy you are concerned about?'

'Miles,' she replied laconically.

'Miles?' he echoed incredulously. 'How on earth can anyone worry about Miles? He is a perfect son in every way, Maria.'

'Yes, in every way but one. He doesn't have a wife, and that makes him a prime target for every single predatory female in the county. I would love to know where he spent this evening.'

'Nonsense, Maria. You really are making a mountain out of a molehill. As he just told you, he simply made some new friends whilst on holiday and gave them a lift home, then out of gratitude they invited him home for supper. Honestly dear, you and your womanly intuition.'

Maria didn't pursue the subject further, for she knew how much Thomas adored his son, and would never hear a word said against him. She also knew Miles had not told her the whole truth. Some of it perhaps, but she was sure he had prevaricated and this was what worried her, for it was the first time she had ever had cause to doubt the word of her son. She was convinced that, somehow, behind all this lay the hand of a woman.

After a week of Miles arriving home late at night, long after supper, and on two successive occasions when everyone had gone to bed. On the Saturday morning, Maria's suspicions were vindicated.

They were all sitting in the dining room having a second cup of tea after breakfast, including Annie and Bull, when during a lull in the conversation, Miles quite unintentionally created somewhat of a furore. 'I have a favour to ask mother. Please may I bring my lady friend to tea tomorrow?'

He could never have imagined his request would have had such a spectacular effect, for Thomas and Bull had just taken rather a large gulp of their tea, and amidst a great deal of coughing and spluttering, they both deposited the whole mess on Maria's crisp white tablecloth in front of them. While Annie, who had been on the point of lifting her cup, sent it crashing down upon the polished hardwood floor, to splinter into a dozen pieces.

'What a stupid time to come out with a statement like that,' bellowed Thomas, amidst the noise and chaos of mopping up operations. 'Look what a mess you caused Annie to make, apart from smashing one of your mother's favourite cups,' he added, wiping his chin and shirt front with a table napkin.

Except for Miles, Maria was the only calm one among them, and suddenly she laughed, that wonderful tinkling sound, which never failed to transport the mind of Thomas back to that beautiful stream he had so unexpectedly discovered one day in his youth in a sheltered glade in the Wolds, chuckling its merry way around pebbles and stones, and immediately he was calm, and the uncharacteristic flash of temper was past.

'I'm sorry I shouted at you son, but you could have given us some small hint about this relationship, and possibly at a more appropriate time perhaps.'

'You should have listened to me, Thomas,' said Maria, with an irritating half smile hovering around the corners of her mouth. 'I warned you last Saturday night and told you then that Miles had changed. Good Lord, he has been singing on his way down to breakfast every morning this week, and staggering home to his bed late at night, long after the birds have gone to roost and, if you failed to recognise those symptoms as a classic example of love sickness, Thomas Cartwright, then all I can say is, you must be feeling your age.'

Miles broke in upon the laughter which ensued after his mother's facetious remarks. 'You still have not given me an answer to my request, mother.'

'Sorry, my dear. Yes, of course you may bring your friend home to tea. What is her name?'

'Ruth. Ruth Myers.'

'What does her father do?' asked Thomas, trying to show a fatherly interest, though still finding it difficult to believe that his son, after all these years of being a confirmed bachelor, had actually invited some lady friend home to tea.

'Her father is dead,' said Miles quietly. 'He died while Ruth was but a child, for she cannot even remember him, consequently she doesn't care to talk about him.'

'Where does Ruth live, darling?' asked Maria in an endeavour to lift the conversation back to its original gaiety.

'None of you will ever believe this,' replied Miles, hugely enjoying his unusual moment of everyone's undivided attention.

'Go on son, try us,' said Thomas, expecting a small terrace house in some murky back street near the docks.

'Well actually,' beamed Miles, a trifle pompously. 'Ruth lives with her mother in a house approximately one mile this side of Hull, the drive of which, you have all passed quite often. Their house is known as The Gables!'

The expressions upon the faces of his companions were of stunned incredulity, as he knew they would be, when he revealed where Ruth lived.

Thomas was the first to find his voice. 'Good Lord, I have seen her coming out of the drive in a trap with her mother. Miles, she is beautiful. How the devil did you manage to attract someone as young and lovely as her?'

'We saw them last month when we drove into Hull. You're right, Thomas, she is a real beauty,' said Bull. 'Don't you remember, Annie? You remarked about her hair and what a lovely girl she was.'

'Oh yes, I remember. My word, Miles, you will be the envy of all the young men in the county if you are seen out with that one.'

Maria was more than a little piqued at being the only one present, who had not seen this vision of loveliness over which they all so ardently enthused. 'Thomas, why did you ask Miles how he could attract someone so young and lovely as this Ruth, you all keep gushing on about?' she asked acidly. 'I mean, he is equally as handsome as you were at his age, if not more so. By the way, how old is your young lady, Miles?'

'Twenty. But very sensible for her age,' he added quickly. He was becoming irritated by all these questions and innuendoes, and suddenly he pushed back his chair and stood up. 'Please excuse me, mother,' he said abruptly.

'Where are you going darling?' asked Maria.

Miles smiled, encompassing the four of them. 'Well if you really want to know, I am spending my day in the country, riding with Ruth. Please do not bother to save any dinner or supper for me tonight. I will see you all again tomorrow.'

When Ruth arrived the following afternoon, Maria was astounded by her beauty, and amazed at the poise extolled in one so young. However, she was like a ray of sunshine, lighting up the dark dusty corners of the old house, and she favourably impressed them all by her sweet and gentle nature.

Much to the chagrin of Miles, Ruth was totally monopolised by his mother and Annie, and he spent most of the afternoon wandering aimlessly along in their wake, as he followed them around the gardens and nearby woods.

He did, however, manage to snatch a few moments alone with her in the conservatory, while the others were organising tea, and Ruth melted into his arms as he held her close and kissed her. 'My dearest. Why do you forsake me and leave me so?' he asked softly, kissing her hair.

'Oh, you silly man,' she replied with a devastating smile. 'I shall never forsake you.

I love you Miles, but your mother also loves you, and if she wishes to drag me away from your side, then perhaps it is only to try and discover what kind of person I am, and if I would be a suitable daughter-in-law.'

Miles stared at this vision of loveliness he held in his arms, hardly daring to believe the words she had just so casually uttered. 'Darling, we have only known each other for a couple of weeks. Did you say daughter-in-law?' he stammered. 'Does that mean we may become engaged, and that one day soon you will marry me?'

She gazed into his eyes, her own wet with tears of happiness. 'Yes Miles we may, and yes, one day soon I will.'

He leapt in the air and shouted with joy, then he picked her up and whirled around, and still holding her thus, his mouth searched hungrily for hers, and as their lips locked together in their first really passionate kiss, Thomas and Maria stepped into the conservatory.

'Oh, oh! You see what these youngsters get up to Maria, immediately our backs are turned,' boomed Thomas.

Completely unabashed, Miles gently put Ruth down, but continued to hold her hand. 'Mother. Father. We have something to tell you. Ruth and I have just become engaged!'

he said euphorically.

Maria was the first to recover. 'Why, that is marvellous darling. Congratulations,' she cried, rushing forward to kiss and embrace the two lovers.

'Engaged!' exploded Thomas. 'But you haven't known each other a month.'

'Oh, Thomas, don't be such an old misery,' interposed Maria. 'If you remember, we only met for one night, and that was sufficient for us to realise we were in love.'

Thomas bowed to Maria's greater wisdom and congratulated the young couple, kissing Ruth and shaking the hand of his son. 'Well, I will say this for you, Miles. You were a few years searching, but you didn't take long in making up your mind when you found Ruth,' joked his father, as Bull and Annie joined them, and were told the splendid news.

'Ruth, does your mother know about this engagement?' asked Thomas, as they were going in for tea.

'No, I'm afraid not. You see it only happened a few moments ago. Neither Miles nor I knew until then.'

'I see. Well son, I think perhaps you should ask Ruth's mother for her permission to become engaged to her daughter, before we embark upon any celebrating.'

Ruth appeared a little crestfallen, but not

the irrepressible Miles. 'All right, father,' he said in a matter of fact voice. 'If you think that is the correct procedure, then it shall be done. Come along my dear,' he added, once again catching hold of Ruth's hand.

'Miles, where are you going?' cried Maria. 'Tea is almost ready.'

Miles turned and smiled. 'Sorry, mother. Tea will have to wait. This is far more important. I am going to ask Mrs Myers if I may become engaged to her lovely daughter. We just might return with her, so it could be advisable to set another place at the table.'

Before Maria could protest, they had gone.

Lucy was ecstatic when she heard the news and willingly gave permission for her daughter to become engaged to Miles, and she was equally enthusiastic in her acceptance of the invitation to return with them to Mount Pleasant for tea.

As they entered the magnificent hall, with its huge coloured glass dome set high in the roof, Lucy looked around her and revelled in the sense and smell of real wealth.

Miles was leading her to the dining room, but a servant intercepted him, and after a few whispered words, he guided them to the drawing room.

As Miles opened the door and ushered in his guests, everyone stood and waited to be introduced, except Maria, she stepped forward, arms outstretched, and embracing Lucy kissed her on both cheeks in true continental fashion.

'Mother, meet Mrs Myers,' said Miles, as he stood between Ruth and her mother.

'Oh no. Not so formal. Please call me Lucy.'

'Very well, Lucy. I am Maria, and this weakling here is Thomas Cartwright, and this other fragile person is Bull Hyde and his adorable wife, Annie.'

Lucy stared in undisguised admiration. She had met many men during her lifetime, but never anyone quite so huge and as powerfully built as these two.

However Lucy was noted for her ready wit and repartee, and quickly found her tongue. 'Yes Maria, I see what you mean. They do both appear to be suffering from rather a bad attack of malnutrition,' she quipped, with a laugh. Her laugh was infectious and they all joined in, even Thomas and Bull, at whom her remark had been aimed.

The expected strain of introducing Ruth's mother into the family circle had evaporated for, with her extrovert personality and rather brash style, reminiscent of her barmaid days, she was an instant success with Annie and Maria.

During tea, Lucy completely dominated the conversation, being the absolute antithesis of her gentle quiet daughter. However, when she continued after tea, Miles saw a distinct advantage in her verbosity, and quietly taking Ruth by the arm, he discreetly guided her through the open French windows and into the garden.

'Gosh, I had no idea your mother could talk so much,' said Miles, as he heaved a sigh of relief.

Ruth laughed. 'Yes, she is inclined to become a little over enthusiastic sometimes. Oh Miles, just smell this, isn't it delicious?' she added, pausing to breathe in the intoxicating scent of honeysuckle, as it spread in apparent luxuriant abandon, over and around the rustic arches, beneath which they were strolling.

He led her to a shady arbour, almost hidden by flourishing shrubs, then producing a clean white handkerchief, he spread it upon the garden seat.

The silence, apart from the humming of bees and the distant song of birds, was complete, and in this typically beautiful, English country garden, on that warm summer evening, the conditions for young lovers, were indescribably idyllic and absolutely perfect.

Sitting down beside his lovely companion, Miles took her in his arms and kissed her. Tentatively at first, but then as the heat rose within him, his kisses became more passionate, and she reciprocated kiss for kiss, passion with passion, until at last he realised, he was on the verge of committing an unforgivable act. The very same act he had found so despicable in Billy and some of his friends of similar ilk, who had fallen to this temptation with dire results, and suddenly, with a low cry of anguish, he broke away.

Ruth sat perfectly still, her beautiful eyes clouded with emotion, her lips moist from his kisses, and a strange look of injured innocence upon her lovely face. 'Darling, why did you stop?' she asked calmly. 'Just when I was really beginning to enjoy your kisses.'

He looked at her askance. She certainly appeared much calmer than he felt, yet he knew she possessed no guile. 'That is precisely the reason I stopped, my dear,' he replied in a rather strained voice, shifting his position slightly, because of a peculiar dull ache in his groin. 'You see darling, we were both enjoying ourselves and, had we continued neither of us would have been satisfied until we had gone all the way.'

'But Miles, that would have been wonderful. I just know it would. Oh! darling, can't we try again. Please?'

He gazed at her wide eyed innocence, and wondered how such a beautiful creature could live in this tawdry world, surrounded by vice, deceit and temptation, yet remain so aloof and completely ignorant of the facts of life. And he marvelled at the way her mother must have protected her since early childhood.

'No, my dear, we cannot try again, as you so succinctly put it.' He spoke slowly, choosing his words carefully. The pain in his groin was easing now and he felt more comfortable, and much more in control of himself. 'My dear Ruth, if we do you could become pregnant, and that would be disastrous, for then we should have to get married.'

Ruth looked puzzled. 'Would that be such a terrible thing Miles? I mean, if we had to get married. You do want to marry me, don't you?'

Once again he was staggered by her naivete, but knew he could not take advantage of it. Holding her closely in his arms, yet carefully avoiding those warm sensuous lips, he forced a hollow sounding laugh. 'Yes my dearest Ruth,' he answered quietly. 'Of course I want to marry you, but there are certain codes of conduct to which we must adhere.'

'What kind of codes?'

'Well, to begin with, we only became engaged today, and I still haven't bought you an engagement ring. Then we are supposed to wait a while before we announce our wedding day.'

'Oh, dear Miles, you make everything sound so complicated, dull and boring,' she replied, as she snuggled closer to him. 'Why can't we get married in the autumn?'

He could feel the heat of her young pliant body through the thin material of her summer dress, and as his senses reeled, he succumbed to her wishes.

Suddenly, he sat bolt upright and, with a great effort, he gently but firmly pushed her away. 'Very well, my darling,' he gasped, the sweat welding his shirt to his back. 'You shall have your way. We will be married in September!'

Ruth flung her arms around his neck and kissed and hugged him. 'Oh! Darling Miles. What a wonderful man you are,' she cried happily. 'I promise, you will never regret this day.'

He eased himself from her all enveloping embrace. 'Come along my dear,' he said, rising to his feet and searching for her hand.

'We shall have to go and ask your mother's permission.'

They burst through the open French windows hand in hand, their features alight with excitement. Everyone was seated just as they had left them, with Lucy continuing to dominate the conversation, while her audience appeared a trifle bemused.

She broke off in mid-sentence, as the two lovers entered. 'Wherever have you been?' she cried accusingly. 'Look at your lovely dress Ruth. It's ruined, and your hair looks as though Miles has pulled you through a hedge backwards.'

Lucy opened her mouth to continue her tirade but, to her utter amazement, her daughter cut her off. 'Mother!' she almost shouted. 'Will you please be quiet, just for once? Miles wishes to speak with you, in private.'

Feeling rather put down, for her daughter had never previously spoken to her in such a manner, Lucy swivelled her eyes from Ruth, and riveted them upon Miles. As did everyone else in the room.

'Mrs Myers,' he began formally. 'Will you please accompany me to the library?'

Without speaking, Lucy rose from her chair and meekly followed him out of the room.

It was a very different Lucy, who returned with Miles five minutes later, and much to the bewilderment of the others, she rushed across the room and embraced her daughter.

'Congratulations, my darling,' she cooed, then dabbing her eyes with a tiny lace handkerchief. 'Oh! Ruth. You have made me so happy.'

Thomas uncoiled himself from his chair. 'I am sorry, but we seem to have missed something,' he said coolly.

Ruth disentangled herself from her mother's arms, and in two strides was standing between him and Maria. 'Oh! Mr and Mrs Cartwright,' she cried, her face radiant with joy. 'Miles has asked me to marry him,' she jumped up and kissed Thomas on the cheek, then bending down, hugged and kissed Maria.

Maria rose to her feet. 'I don't really understand what all the excitement is about,' she said patiently. 'Less than an hour ago, Miles and Ruth announced their engagement. Well, I was always under the impression, that when a couple became engaged, the ultimate result would eventually be marriage. So what is the cause of all this furore?'

Lucy, forever on the lookout for an opening, willingly stepped in. 'Terribly sorry, Maria. I was a bit overwhelmed by the news myself, and wasn't thinking properly. Miles and Ruth, wish to be married on the third of September!'

'Third of September?' echoed four of her listeners.

'I presume you mean this September?' asked Maria, sitting down again.

'Yes of course,' replied Lucy, her features almost as flushed and radiant as those of her daughter's.

'But that is less than six weeks away,' cried Maria, after a quick mental calculation. 'We shall never have everything ready in time.'

'I know it is less than six weeks away, but such is the impetuosity of the youth of today,' replied Lucy grandly. 'Don't you worry about a thing Maria. I will make sure all is ready for the big day,' she added confidently.

★ ★ ★

As Thomas stood outside the church with the rest of the wedding party, waiting for the man to set up his cumbersome looking apparatus, to enable him to make images of the group. His mind was transported back to that other time he had walked from this same church, with his lovely Kate beside him, all those years ago.

Poignantly he thought of the happiness surrounding them on that memorable sun kissed day. Then he remembered the golden haired little boy stumbling over the graves, shouting. 'Papa, papa.' He could almost hear him now, his childlike high pitched voice, pushing back the curtains of time.

Someone placed a hand upon his arm, breaking his train of thought, and a voice said. 'Come along, father, that photographer is asking you to smile.'

This was a man's voice, and Thomas stole a glance at him, for this was the little boy of whom he had just been thinking. He was a man now of some thirty years, standing tall and proud beside him, only three inches shorter than himself, and almost as broad, and he had just witnessed him marry one of the most beautiful young women he had ever seen.

Thomas uttered a silent prayer. *Dear God. Bestow upon my son a happy marriage, and please allow him to enjoy far more years of married bliss than I had with my beloved Kate.*

Quite suddenly the prolonged photo session was over and, amid much cheering and waving, the happy couple strolled hand in hand through a sea of rose petals, to their waiting coach.

The bride and groom, followed by their guests, headed a convoy of similar assorted vehicles out of town towards the country, ultimately turning into the drive of The Gables, where a sumptuous wedding feast awaited them. When the meal and all the speeches were finally concluded, Lucy informed the guests that, if they so wished, they could go along to the drawing room, where all the presents were on display.

Sometime later, Thomas was wandering a little aimlessly around the room, admiring a magnificent array of gifts, when he casually picked up a silver snuff box, and enjoying the feel of the smooth precious metal and its obvious antiquity, he idly turned it over.

Thomas froze, and uttered a gasp of amazement, as the ever present ever watchful Maria was instantly by his side.

'What is it, Thomas?' she asked, concerned as she saw the pallor beneath his tan.

'Follow me!' he rasped, as he made a fist, hiding the box from the prying eyes of any fellow guest. Maria followed him through another door further down the hall and, after she had entered, he closed it softly behind them, then strode over to the window. Opening his hand, he turned the inanimate object over, and pointing to the back of it, exclaimed. 'What are those?'

238

Maria peered at the deep furrows scratched into the metal. 'They appear to be letters,' she replied. 'Yes, they are letters. Someone's initials no doubt.'

'Yes, yes, I know that, but what are those letters, and whose initials are they?' he demanded impatiently.

Maria scrutinised the box more closely. 'TC,' she said slowly, her heart going cold with a feeling of some unknown impending tragedy. 'Thomas Cartwright!' she finally whispered. 'Oh! Thomas, what does it mean?'

'I don't know Maria, not yet anyway, but I certainly intend to find out. I scratched my initials on this snuff box just after my parents died, when I went to live with Aunt Lottie. I should remember, because she gave me the biggest hiding of my life, for disfiguring her precious silver snuff box.'

'What are you going to do, Thomas,' Maria asked apprehensively.

'Get to the bottom of this immediately. Go tell Miles I wish to see him.' His tone was more a command than a request. She hesitated. 'Go now woman!' he shouted at her.

Maria whirled on him, the fiery passion of her Latin ancestors rising within her, with her colour heightened by the rush of blood, and her eyes flashing, she stood her ground. 'Don't you shout at me Thomas Cartwright,' she hissed. 'And don't ever call me woman again, and if you spoil this day for our son and his new bride because of some silly old snuff box, I shall walk out and never speak to you again!'

Maria was exhausted after her verbal outburst, and trembling, she waited for the explosion which she knew was bound to come, for no man had ever dared to speak to Thomas in that vein, never mind a slip of a woman like herself.

However, no eruption followed her scathing remarks. In fact her words seemed to have had the opposite effect, for quite suddenly Thomas appeared much calmer, and he was once again in complete control of himself.

'Sorry Maria. I had no right to speak to you like that. None of this is your doing, and I apologise for dragging you into it. I also promise not to spoil our son's wedding day, but somehow I must discover the truth of this matter. So please my dearest Maria, go now and bring Miles to me.'

Much mollified by the change in his attitude towards her, Maria acquiesced, and returned a few moments later with her son.

'Hello, father,' said Miles, surprise in his voice. 'Whatever are you and mother doing in here? You should be out there mixing with the guests.'

Thomas ignored his son's remarks. 'Come over here, Miles, by the window, I wish to show you something.'

'What is it, father?' he asked nonchalantly, pretending not to notice the firm set of his father's jaw, or the worried frown creasing his brow.

Thomas opened his hand and revealed the silver box, lying in the centre of his palm. 'Tell me son,' he said quietly, painfully aware Maria was hovering close by, listening and watching his every move. 'Where did this come from?'

Miles smiled and sighed with relief. 'Oh, that old snuff box. It is something Ruth gave me as an extra wedding present. Why do you ask?'

'Do you happen to know how it came to be in Ruth's possession?' Thomas persisted.

'Yes, of course. Her father left it, along with all his other things to her mother, and Lucy passed it on to Ruth.'

The lines around the mouth of Thomas tightened, as he fought for self control. 'You may return to your guests now, Miles,' he said, his voice so cold and devoid of any emotion, Maria involuntarily clutched at her chair. 'Please ask Lucy to come and see me,' he added as Miles reached the door.

Lucy came in, all bounce and frills, excited that her beloved daughter had succeeded in catching such a wonderfully marriageable man as Miles Cartwright.

'Oh, Maria,' she gushed ecstatically. 'What a truly delicious wedding party this is.'

Thomas stepped forward. 'Sorry to prize you away from your guests Lucy, but this is rather important. Can you please tell me how you came to own this snuff box?'

Suddenly Lucy's mantle of gaiety faded, as her eyes filled with sadness. 'Yes, certainly. It was among my late husband's possessions, and naturally came to me when he died.'

'I see,' Thomas replied. 'Now I know your name is Mrs Myers, but what was your husband's name Lucy?'

Though his voice was smooth as a silken thread, the question was totally unexpected and, for the first time, the woman sensed something was wrong. She hesitated. 'I'm waiting Lucy,' he said gently.

She found it impossible to drag her eyes away from those twin points of blue steel boring into her own, and she had the awful feeling her innermost thoughts were being bared and probed, by her giant inquisitor. 'Very well, I will tell you,' she stammered.

'For some reason, which he would never

discuss, even though we were properly married, he forced me to keep my maiden name. *His name was Butlin. Charlie Butlin*!'

If Lucy had expected her revelation to have some dire effect upon her listeners, she was disappointed, for neither of them moved a muscle. Of course, she had no way of knowing, but Thomas and Maria were rooted to the spot, utterly immobilised by those few terrible, soul destroying words.

The cacophony of sound from the wedding party reached a new crescendo, and seemed to be battering down the door of this otherwise silent room. As no one spoke, Lucy, regaining her confidence continued. 'Regarding the silver snuff box, it was in an old tin trunk along with some other stuff, and there was a card with it, which said. *'For Charles, when he is twenty one years old. With all my love, Mother'*.'

As though in a daze, Thomas gripped the back of a chair and eased himself around it, to sink gratefully down upon the seat, while Maria moved swiftly to the side of Lucy and guided her firmly towards the door.

'Steady on, Maria,' she remonstrated. 'What did I say? I only told him what he wanted to know.'

Maria tightened her grip upon Lucy's arm, and practically forced her out of the room.

'Please go and attend to your guests, dear,' she said persuasively.

Immediately the door closed, Maria rushed across the room to Thomas and fell upon her knees, burying her head in his lap.'Oh, my poor darling. Whatever shall we do?'

Thomas however, was paying no heed to what his mistress was saying. He appeared to be staring straight ahead, at some fixed point on the opposite wall, while absent-mindedly stroking her hair.

He was thinking, delving deep into the far reaches of his memory, to that day when he and Kate met for the first time. When they were returning from their memorable picnic, how violently his Aunt Lottie had reacted to the suggestion from William, that they should have a day out visiting Watersmeet.

The thought of that village flashed his mind forward, to a whole kaleidoscope of blurred images and sounds, which had lain dormant in his subconscious, and had become almost lost in the mists of time.

He saw once again the tall three storey house, William had ordered to be built as a surprise for Lottie, the house she had adamantly refused to enter, in fact had never even seen, simply because it was situated at Watersmeet. *But why?*

Then, again leaping forward in time, it

was that terrible day of the explosion, when his life had been devastated, and his entire family wiped out, in the carnage which had engulfed the *Elizabeth Kate*.

With his tortured mind lifting a corner of the fine veil, cobwebbed by time, separating his conscious from his subconscious, he was now standing in the village street, beside a cart containing the dead bodies of his beloved children, and the pathetic remains of his once vibrant beautiful Kate.

He heard a voice, faint at first, then more clearly: '*Hello Charlie. I saw you earlier today, running out of the churchyard.*'

Then a woman's voice: '*I saw him an'all, running up the street like a bat out of hell!*'

A few seconds later, another woman's voice: '*He reached the hill top gate just as the ship blew up, and hung on the top rail screaming, 'No! No!'*'

Thomas closed his eyes tight, as a terrible shudder ripped through his massive frame, and instantly Maria was on her feet, her arms around him.

'Oh my darling! What is it?' she asked in a hoarse whisper.

At first Thomas did not reply. He seemed to be coming out of some kind of trance. Then, very slowly, he eased himself into an upright position and gently kissed her. She was shocked by his next remark.

'*Please Maria, promise you will never leave me.*'

His voice sounded different, as though somehow he had aged during the previous fifteen minutes, and she pressed her cheek close to his. 'Thomas, what a strange remark to make. Of course I will never leave you. For without you my dearest, life would have no meaning and I should most certainly die.'

Her reply seemed to comfort him, and when he spoke again his voice was stronger and more firm, as he slowly recovered from the trauma he had just experienced. Gently removing her arms from around his neck, he stood up and stared unseeingly out of the window. 'You do realise the implications of all this, don't you, Maria?' he asked, turning and once again picking up the ill-fated snuff box.

'Not entirely. No. I know it has something to do with Ruth's father, but I'm not sure what.'

'This means my dear. Our son has married the daughter of that murderous swine Charlie Butler, whom Bull and I drowned in the River Tagus, and whose father I had previously killed in a fight, which makes me the killer of my daughter-in-law's father and also her grandfather!'

'No! Thomas,' cried Maria, linking a reassuring arm through his. 'You know very well Jed Butler died in a fair fight, and his death was an unfortunate accident. Anyway, you acted more in self defence against an arrogant bully, rather than in anger.'

Maria then remembered how she and Annie had urged him to seek revenge upon the vile creature who had destroyed his family. 'As for Charlie Butler, you had no option other than to seek out and annihilate him, after what he did to poor Kate and your lovely children. So please my darling, don't you be having any qualms about cleansing the world of scum like those two, for neither of them was worth a sailor's spit. By the way Thomas, you never mentioned your scratched initials on that snuff box to either Lucy or Miles.'

'I know. Perhaps I was too ashamed.'

Maria stared at him. 'Too ashamed,' she echoed. 'What on earth have you ever done to be ashamed of?'

'Not for myself,' he replied quietly. 'For Aunt Lottie!'

He placed a finger upon her lips, as she opened her mouth to speak. 'You see Maria. I think that when William broke off their engagement, Jed Butler caught her on the rebound and they had an affair, the result of which was a baby boy named Charles!'

She recoiled from him, and was now clinging to the back of a chair. 'You must be mad Thomas. How can you possibly think, your dear sweet Aunt would ever stoop so low?'

'I know Maria, the very thought of those two together appals and revolts me, yet all the facts point to some kind of illicit collusion.'

'Facts? What facts?' she cried imperiously.

He could see she was riled, and secretly admired her for leaping so staunchly to the defence of his late Aunt. 'Well, to begin with, there is this benighted snuff box and the card signed Mother. How else could they possibly have been found among Charlie's effects, unless Aunt Lottie had given them to his father?'

He then proceeded to tell her of his other fears, and the fragments of conversation he had remembered hearing, on that dreadful day at Watersmeet.

'You do understand what you are implying, don't you, Thomas?' She had turned pale as he unfolded his horrendous tale of intrigue and premeditated murder, and was gripping the back of her chair so hard, her knuckles shone white.

'Yes, Maria, I understand. If all I am saying is true, and I have no cause to doubt the authenticity of my reasoning, then unknowingly, until it was too late, *Charlie Butler murdered his own mother!*'

Maria was silent a moment, her mind in a turmoil. 'What do you mean, Thomas, unknowingly, until it was too late?' she asked abruptly.

'Remember I told you George Teanby saw Charlie running out of the churchyard, and then that woman who saw him clinging to the hill top gate screaming, No, No, just as the explosion occurred? Well, I think that somehow he suspected that village had been his place of birth, and visited the church to verify his suspicions.'

'All of this sounds terribly hypothetical, Thomas, but supposing, I am not saying you are mind, but just supposing you are right in all these assumptions, what can you possibly do, to prove any of your far fetched theories?'

His reply came sharp and crisp, as though he had already anticipated her question. 'Go to the church at Watersmeet tomorrow!' he answered glibly.

Maria sat down upon the chair, her

brow puckered, deep in thought. After a long silence, she spoke again. 'My dearest Thomas,' her voice was quiet and soothing. 'All of this happened so long ago, and I know it is part of your life, but everyone is dead and gone now. Please don't allow these voices from the past to haunt you, my dear. If we do visit that church tomorrow, and if all you say is proved to be true. What good will come of it?'

'Probably no good at all Maria,' he replied gently. 'But this is something I must do, if only to settle so many unanswered questions which have arisen over the years. I am determined to find out one way or another, and whatever the outcome, at least we shall have tried to discover the truth of this distasteful matter, and I may even have some peace of mind.'

Maria realised he would brook no argument regarding his visit to Watersmeet tomorrow, and decided there was nothing she could say or do which would cause him to change his mind, so with an audible sigh of resignation, she rose to her feet. 'Shall we join the others, Thomas?' she asked with a faint smile.

He followed her out of the room, and returned the cause of all his accusations and subsequent revelations, to its rightful place among the other wedding presents.

As they mixed with the other guests, any casual observer looking at Thomas, would never have suspected the trauma he had so recently suffered, and as he and Maria strolled around the garden, she with her arm linked through his, they suddenly came face to face with Miles and his beautiful bride.

My God, thought Thomas. How the devil could a scurrilous villain like Charlie Butler, father such a vision of loveliness as Ruth?

The voice of Miles cut across his line of thought. 'Hello you two. I'm pleased to see you have decided to leave that stuffy old room, and take a breath of fresh air.'

Maria was filled with admiration for the prodigious self-control Thomas manifested, as Ruth stepped forward and, standing on her tiptoes, reached up and kissed him on the cheek. 'Thank you, father, for helping to make this such a wonderful day for us,' she cooed happily. 'I can call you father, can't I?' she asked impulsively.

To hear the daughter of that evil bastard call him father, was an obscenity and absolute anathema to Thomas, and it was only because of his earlier promise to Maria, that he would not spoil this day for their son, he managed, albeit with a superhuman effort, to control himself

251

and actually smile, as he replied in the affirmative.

He and Maria sought out Luke Carlton and his wife, for Miles had invited them along with Billy's wife and family, so of course Thomas had to have a few words with his old friend about farming, the price of stock and the world in general.

'By heck, Thomas, she be a fine lass that lad of yours has got himself hitched to,' remarked Luke, as they were parting.

'Yes. Thank you, Luke,' Thomas replied as they moved away.

At that moment, amid much excitement and gaiety, everyone flooded out of the house to watch the happy couple boarding their coach, which was standing on the drive, waiting to take them on the first part of their journey to Venice, for a three week honeymoon.

Thomas had to admit this wife of his son's really was a beautiful girl, as she stood there beside Miles, elegantly dressed in her trousseau, and looking every inch the wife of an English country gentleman. Even so, he had great difficulty in suppressing a feeling of abhorrence, as he stooped to kiss her and wish them both bon-voyage.

* * *

Early the next morning, Thomas and Maria boarded the ferry bound for New Holland, and after a smooth crossing, led their horses onto the pier.

After a long uneventful ride, during which very little conversation had taken place between them, and Maria had suffered a strong sense of foreboding, they rode down the main street of Watersmeet, straight to the church.

As they dismounted and were about to tie the two horses to a post by the lychgate, the vicar appeared in the church porch. Handing the reins of his horse to Maria, Thomas strode down the path to have a word with the minister.

'Good day to you, vicar,' he said in greeting.

'Good day to you, sir,' the man replied affably. 'Can I be of any assistance? You appear to have travelled a long way this morning?'

Thomas smiled ruefully as he shook the dust off his hacking jacket, then dusted down his riding breeches and boots. 'Yes we have. From Kingston-upon-Hull, actually. Tell me vicar, do you keep a record book of all baptisms that are performed in your church, and if so, may we see it please?'

'Indeed we do, and yes of course you

may.' He turned to greet Maria, for she had secured the horses, and had now joined the two men.

'Follow me please, and I will show you the book.' He led them into the church and through to a small room at the back. Opening a cupboard, he withdrew a large, old book, and after blowing off the dust, placed it upon the table with a flourish.

'There you are sir. I will leave you to peruse the records together. Please return it to the cupboard when you have finished.'

Thomas waited until the vicar had left the room then, with a sense of suppressed excitement, he moved forward.

Maria however, was quicker, and leaping across the small room, she placed her hands on top of the still closed book. 'Are you quite sure, you wish to go ahead with this stupid macabre investigation, and to learn what is written within these pages?'

Thomas gently but firmly removed her hands, then lifting her with one arm around her waist, he moved her aside and, without speaking, he opened the book and began flicking through the pages, searching for the year in which he surmised Charlie would have been born.

Suddenly, with a cry more of agony, than of triumph, he pointed. 'There it is Maria!'

The finely written words seemed to leap out at him from the crowded page.

March 15th. 1825. A son born to Lottie Cartwright of Kingston-upon-Hull. Father, Jed Butler of the same town.

They both stared, as though hypnotised by this all revealing message from the past, until Thomas, with a half sob, half groan, slammed the book shut, and flinging it to the back of the cupboard, he banged the door to.

Gripping Maria by the arm, he marched her out of the room and out of the church, until halfway down the path, he came to an abrupt halt. 'Sorry about that Maria. I just had to get out of there. Come with me please,' he added, as he released her.

He made his way across the churchyard, carefully avoiding the grassed over mounds, towards a secluded spot situated in the far corner, stopping at the foot of three very small graves, containing the bodies of his children and the pitiful remains of his beloved wife.

'I am so sorry Kate,' he said in a low whisper. 'Please forgive me. I had no idea who he was. I know that is no excuse. I should have done more to find out.' His final words trailed off into oblivion, as his voice broke and deep sobs racked his huge frame, and Maria, her cheeks wet with tears, led him gently away.

No words passed between them as they rode slowly up the street towards High House and, as they drew level with George Teanby's workshop, Thomas glanced in the yard and saw a stranger working there, for old George had passed on two years ago.

Riding that short distance, was akin to running a gauntlet of bad memories for, as they reached the hilltop gate and glimpsed the river below, Thomas had a vivid recollection of that awful day, and saw once again the burning hulk of the *Elizabeth Kate*.

Maria leaned over and grasped the bridle of his horse, leading him forward, for Thomas had stopped and was staring down the hill. 'Come along, dear,' she said in a light hearted way, trying to lift the gloom which seemed to lay so heavily upon him. 'This is not good for you, and will in no way help you to cope with this latest development.'

Willingly, Thomas followed her lead and together they rode into the yard adjacent to High House.

A middle-aged man was busy toiling in the garden and, as they dismounted he straightened his back, thrust his spade into the well tilled soil and walked towards them. 'Good day to you sir,' he said as he touched his cap. 'It's good to see you, and you too ma'am,' he added, turning to Maria.

A heavily built masculine looking woman, her hair flecked with grey, appeared at the front door. 'Well, bless my soul, if it isn't Master Thomas and his lady come to visit. Good day to you sir, and to you my lady,' the woman said, wiping her hands upon her apron. 'Do come inside, sir, and I'll make you both a nice hot cup of tea.'

'Thank you, Mrs Clements. That would be much appreciated,' replied Thomas with a quick smile, amazing Maria by his resilience at recovering, outwardly at least, from the shock he had so recently suffered.

'Bring our sandwiches Maria, we will have lunch in the room at the top. Will that be all right with you Mrs Clements?'

'Of course, sir,' she replied, her ready smile hiding the fact how much she hated climbing all those stairs.

As they entered that top floor room, Thomas emitted a gasp of surprise. 'Look Maria. On the table.'

Maria gave a cry of delight, for standing in the centre of the table was a highly polished brass bell, and embossed around the rim were the words: '*Elizabeth Kate.*'

'Now how the devil did that get there?'

257

asked a puzzled Thomas.

'I have no idea. Perhaps Mrs Clements will enlighten us, when she arrives with the tea,' replied Maria, seating herself upon the single bed and nonchalantly swinging her legs. 'What a lovely room this is, dear. One feels so far removed from the troubles and tribulations, of the everyday world down below.'

At that moment, there was a light knock on the door and the housekeeper entered, carrying a tray laden with a pot of tea, best china cups, milk and a jug of fresh thick cream to complement two huge slices of apple pie.

'Ah, Mrs Clements,' began Thomas, reluctantly dragging his gaze from the laden tray. 'Can you tell me how this bell comes to be here?'

'Why certainly, sir. One of the village men found it sticking out of the mud, when he was down on the foreshore shooting wild geese. Anyway, he realised it was off your ship, so he brought it here. My, what a mess it was, all caked up with mud and green stuff, but when I cleaned it up I thought it was worth a good polish, and I've given it one every week since. Also the telescope an' all sir.'

'Telescope? What telescope?'

'That one there, sir, on the window ledge behind you.'

Thomas turned around and there was William's favourite telescope. Thomas had obviously forgotten he had used it previously when he was here, though he had sometimes wondered over the years, what had become of it. Now he thought William must have brought it here to admire the view from this window, and here it had remained.

Thrusting a hand in his pocket, Thomas drew forth a sovereign. 'Please give this coin to the man who found the bell, Mrs Clements,' he said, as he handed it to the housekeeper.

'Yes, thank you sir, and I'll tell you now, he'll be most grateful, that he will sir.'

Thomas smiled. 'Thank you, Mrs Clements. That will be all.'

'My word, she goes on a bit,' said Maria, when she knew the subject of her remark was halfway down the stairs.

'Who, Mrs Clements? Don't you worry your pretty head about her darling. She just likes to hear her own voice. Anyway, she's harmless enough. Now how about pouring your old lover a cup of tea,' mumbled Thomas, through a mouthful of cold beef sandwich.

After the meal, Thomas left the table,

and lowering himself onto the edge of the magnificent leather chair William had installed, he picked up the telescope and, leaning forward, adjusted it to bring into focus the foreshore far below.

He sat there for some time, shifting his position occasionally, as he trawled the river bank, and though Maria knew not for what he was searching, she could hazard a shrewd guess.

Eventually however, the early start and the long ride that morning, coupled with the warm Autumn sun as it slanted through that high window, began to take their effect. Placing his telescope upon the windowsill, Thomas eased his tired body into the luxurious depths of his chair, and within two minutes had slipped into a deep sleep.

When Maria was satisfied her lover was fast asleep, she quietly gathered up the tea things and softly closed the door, as she left the room.

Meanwhile, Thomas was having a most unusual experience, for he began to dream, and this was certainly most unusual, for he had never had a dream in his life, and had often been heard to mention the fact.

Now, however, he floated out of that top floor window and found himself walking along the foreshore far below. The day was bright, filled with brilliant sunshine, and yet a mist seemed to hang over the river. Suddenly he made out the ghostly shape of the Elizabeth Kate anchored close to the bank, and coming towards him was the figure of a woman, with a child holding each of her hands.

As the three gossamer figures drifted closer, the woman softly called his name. 'Thomas,' and the two children called in faint haunting voices. 'Papa. Papa.'

In a trice, Thomas had bounded forward, and she was in his arms. 'Oh Kate, Kate, my wonderful, beautiful Kate,' he cried as he kissed her. 'And you. My two lovely children, Elizabeth and Jon,' he said, as he released Kate, to lift each child and hug them.

'Papa, will you take us to the maze on the hilltop, please?'

Before Thomas could reply, the children had each entwined a hand in his, and with Kate in the lead, the four of them floated swiftly and silently, ever upwards until finally dropping gently to earth right at the entrance to the maze.

Still holding his hands, they led him around the intricate paths cut out of the grass sod, shouting and laughing, while Kate sat upon the raised bank, clapping and calling encouragement.

What surprised Thomas, was the sight of several people walking by, none of whom seemed to notice, as though they couldn't see them, or hear the noise from his exuberant children.

Eventually, Elizabeth and Jon seemed to tire of this game, and suddenly Thomas was once again standing on the river bank, holding his children's hands and kissing his wife.

'Goodbye, my beloved, I will wait for you,' she murmured, then began drifting slowly towards the ship, taking his son and daughter with her.

He tried to run after them, but discovered to his horror he couldn't move! 'Kate, Kate,' he shouted, but to no avail, for by now the three of them had almost disappeared, swallowed up in the all pervading mist which surrounded the hull of the Elizabeth Kate.

He awoke with a start, to find Maria gently shaking him by the shoulder, and as if from a great distance, saying, 'Thomas, Thomas, please wake up.'

Slowly, as in a trance, he turned towards her, and in that split second of time, which seemed to stretch to infinity, Maria's world came crashing down, for instinctively she knew she had lost him.

The seeds of doubt, had been sown as

she entered the room and heard Kate's name upon his lips, but now that seed was manifestly propagated for, as she looked more closely, she could see the light of his love, which had enabled her to live in the back street of his life during the twelve years of his marriage to Kate, and which had shone like a beacon for so long, had suddenly been extinguished.

She began to go weak at the knees, and involuntarily grasped the back of his chair as she felt her life's blood drain from her face, but incredibly Thomas didn't seem to notice her obvious distress, or even the pallor of her countenance.

An overwhelming sensation of absolute peace and utter contentment had overtaken the body and spirit of Thomas, and he actually smiled as he spoke to the anguished Maria standing beside him. 'I had a wonderful refreshing sleep Maria. I think it must be this room that has such a peaceful effect upon me.'

His voice sounded weird and detached, like someone speaking from the depths of a darkened cave. He thought Maria might laugh at him, if he told her of his extraordinary meeting with Kate, so he simply used the room as an excuse for something to say.

Maria stared at him, the blood of her ancestors rising within her, and not allowing her to go down without a fight. 'My God! Thomas, you must think I'm completely stupid,' she snapped, as she angrily brushed away the tears with the sleeve of her dress.

'You have never lied to me before, so why lie to me now?'

He opened his mouth to speak, but she silenced him with her next outburst. 'Your refreshing sleep as you call it, had nothing to do with this room, had it? Go on, tell me the truth, lover!' her words dripped with acid.

Thomas remained silent, stunned by her savage verbal assault, and after a moment Maria continued. 'Very well, I will tell you. You had a wonderful dream, during which you were on the bank of the Humber. There you just happened to bump into your precious Kate, who of course still looks just as young and lovely as she did the day you married her! Am I right?' she asked imperiously.

Thomas sat frozen to his chair. His lips moved but no sound came. He was astounded by the uncanny intuitive powers of perception, possessed by this woman who had been his lover for as long as he could remember.

'Am I?' she repeated inexorably.

'Yes,' he replied in an awe-struck whisper. 'But you missed something. You see Elizabeth and Jon were with her!'

Maria laughed, a loud hysterical horrible kind of laugh. 'You great big stupid fool!' she shrieked at him. 'They are all dead and buried years ago, though there wasn't much left of poor Kate to bury,' she finished on a more sombre note.

She saw the shock and the hurt in his eyes, and was immediately filled with compassion. 'I am so sorry Thomas, I should never have said those things to you, however you must realise my dear, this was only a dream.'

'No, Maria. It was more than a dream, much much more.' He had regained his composure now, and was almost speaking in his normal voice. 'Look,' he said, standing up and peering out the window. 'There is still a good hour of daylight left. Come with me and I will prove to you, what I experienced this afternoon was verging on the paranormal.'

Silently, she followed him downstairs and out onto the road, then turning right he led her to the hilltop gate, and after closing it behind them, he walked straight to the entrance of the maze.

He turned towards her, and her heart sank as she saw once again that same distant, detached look she had noticed earlier, and though he seemed composed, she could sense the wave of suppressed excitement shimmering through his huge frame.

'Now, you know I have never in my life been here before. Equally you are well aware, I have never seen this maze, at least not in this world, as we know it. Do you agree with these facts?'

Maria nodded in silent affirmation, and though the evening was warm, she suddenly experienced a chill sweep through her body, and involuntarily drew the shawl more closely around her shoulders.

'Right, watch me Maria, and tell me if I make a mistake.'

He turned from her, and lifting his head high, stepped down onto the well worn paths of the maze. So he continued, striding purposefully the torturous route, twisting and turning, and never for a moment lowering his eyes. When he reached the centre, he looked across at Maria, and in a childlike way, he lifted his hand and waved to her, then turned around and, never faltering, he simply walked out again as though guided by an invisible hand.

When he rejoined Maria and sat down beside her on the soft grass of the bank, she pretended to be unimpressed. 'Yes, quite a demonstration, but it doesn't prove anything. I bet anyone can walk round that.'

'All right, Maria. You try.'

Without a word, she rose to her feet, brushed down her crumpled dress and moved towards the entrance path. Carefully she placed one dainty foot in front of the other, but before she was halfway round, she had become hopelessly lost, and in a fit of pique, stamped her foot, and crossing the paths she ran to the bank and rejoined Thomas.

'Very well Thomas Cartwright,' she pouted. 'Being as you're so damn clever, tell me how you accomplished going around the stupid thing.'

To his credit, Thomas didn't patronise her, or even smile sardonically. No, his look was more of pity, as a vicar would probably bestow upon an unbeliever, which only served to infuriate her all the more.

'I don't suppose for one moment that you will believe me, but as I told you earlier. I was with Kate and the children this afternoon, and even though my body was sitting in that leather chair by the window, my spirit or something was somehow transported out here, and I spent a long while running around this maze with Elizabeth and Jon.'

He was deadly serious, and Maria could see he never for a moment looked upon any of this as some figment of his imagination, or even as a dream. No, he obviously firmly believed, these things had taken place and had actually happened to him.

'What other explanation can there possibly be for the demonstration I gave you just now?' he asked abruptly.

Maria was silent. She had no answer to the way in which he had conquered the many twists and turns of that damned maze with such consummate ease, and his remarks about the children had somehow frightened her.

The sun had dipped below the distant horizon, and the night was turning cool. Again she shivered. 'Come along Thomas, let's go home. We have had a long day, and I'm tired out,' she said wearily as she stood up and began walking towards the gate.

However, that night Maria had another shock awaiting her, for after supper they retired to their room on the middle floor, and Thomas began to gather his night attire and toilet requisites together. 'Thomas, what are you doing?' she asked tremulously.

'I am very sorry Maria. Tonight, I must sleep in the room upstairs. For after my reconciliation with Kate and the children, my conscience will not allow me to share your bed again!' and before she could reply, he had gone.

Maria stood in the centre of the room, shook rigid by those few brief words, while she slowly assimilated the full impact of her lover's parting remarks.

They had been lovers for more than a quarter of a century, and this would be the first time they had slept apart through their long and sometimes turbulent relationship, except of course during the years of his marriage. Slowly, and almost automatically she began to undress, and when she finally crept into the vast double bed, in stunned exasperation she smote the soft pillow with her small fists.

Though Maria slept very little that night, she shed no tears and, as she tossed and turned throughout the long hours, occasionally she spoke her thoughts aloud. 'Oh! My sweet gentle Thomas, why have you done this to me? Damn you Kate. Damn you Lottie, and most of all, Damn you William Earnshaw, for building this stupid house. I should never have allowed you Thomas, to have brought me here yesterday, then none of this would have happened. How can you, the love of my life, who I always thought possessed a superior intelligence to the rest of men, allow some silly fantasy you met in a dream, to come between us and tear us apart like this. Oh! Dear God, what have I ever done to deserve treatment such as this?'

However, there was no answer to her heartfelt plea, from this darkened room, and she pushed herself ever deeper into the mass of the huge feather bed, until finally, through sheer exhaustion, she fell into a troubled sleep.

Maria awoke with a start as light flooded the room, for Thomas had drawn back the curtains and was now standing by her bed, with a cup of tea in his hand.

'Good morning, Maria,' he said genially. 'Time to get up.'

She struggled to a sitting position, and relieved him of the cup. 'What time is it?' she asked, smothering a yawn and rubbing the sleep from her eyes.

'Just after eight. You look worn out. Didn't you sleep very well?'

'What do you think, or even care, after what you did last night, how I slept?' she snapped, as her sleep befuddled brain cleared and the hurtful memory of the previous evening returned.

She saw the line of his mouth tighten as his eyes shut her out, and he moved over to the window. 'Mr Clements keeps the garden looking well, my dear,' he said, totally ignoring her outburst, or her reference to the previous evening.

However, Maria was not beaten yet. 'Thomas, please come here a moment.' Her voice was soft and warm as a gentle summer breeze, and as it floated towards him and washed over him, he turned.

She had removed her night-dress and was leaning backwards, her arms spread along the top of the bed rail. She lifted a hand and cradled her naked breast and, though she had long since lost the bloom of youth, her body was still slim and supple, and her skin satin smooth.

'*Remember these, Thomas?*' She was taunting him now, but Maria was feeling desperate and her womanly charms were the only weapon she had. She moved closer, catlike across the room, and lifting her leg, placed a pretty foot upon a chair, then seductively began to stroke the inside of her thigh.

'Come here,' she purred. 'Just caress me, as only you know how.' She slapped her thigh. 'Come along Thomas. This is warm human flesh, the real genuine article, not some transparent hallucinatory being, from a shadowy spirit world.'

Thomas averted his eyes from this alluring

temptress before him, so blatantly offering her wares, and with a stifled moan, he fled from the room.

'You stupid fool!' Maria screamed after him, as he retreated up the spiral stairs to his room. 'That's right, run up there to your dream fantasy, and just see what satisfaction she will give you,' she shouted, as she stepped back into the room and slammed the door to.

As Maria began to dress, gradually her fury abated, and she started to think more rationally of recent events. She remembered the expression on the face of Thomas, when he saw his initials scratched on the back of that wretched snuff box, and his silent all-consuming anger after he discovered where it had come from.

Then she recalled their ride here to Watersmeet, only to find that his beloved Aunt Lottie had embarked upon a disastrous affair with Jed Butler, the result of which was the man who had unknowingly plotted her hideous destruction, along with Kate and her two children. Now the final humiliation Thomas had suffered, was the fact that their son had fallen in love, and had somehow become ensnared in a marriage to the daughter of that despicable beast, as though he was reaching out and still taking revenge for the death of his father, even from the grave.

As Maria thought of the terrible revelations which had been made to Thomas, all within the space of a few hours, her features softened and her heart went out to him, as she realised the full impact of the trauma he must be suffering, and that somehow his troubled mind must have invented the materialisation of his dead wife and family.

The unexplained incident of his undoubted conquest of the maze, she conveniently pushed to the back of her mind, and completely forgot.

Maria took one last look at herself through the mirror, and apparently satisfied with her reflection, made her way downstairs to the dining room.

He was sitting at the table, tucking into a mountain of fried eggs and bacon, a monster sized mug of steaming hot tea beside him, and as she entered the room he looked up. 'Good morning, Maria,' he mumbled jovially, through a mouthful of bacon and fried bread. 'Did you sleep well, darling?'

She stared at him in amazement. Obviously he had no recollection of the fact that he had visited her earlier that morning, or did he simply wish to forget it? For that brief moment, as she looked at him, time seemed to stand still, as he sat there so intent upon enjoying his breakfast, and that quite ordinary domestic scene became etched upon her memory for all time.

In the same heart beat, she realised through her own stupidity and complete lack of understanding, she had come within a hair's breadth of losing him, and now decided it was help he needed and not retribution. Only time and her own unselfish love, could bring them both back from the edge of this abyss so that, sometime in the future, they might return once more to their normal relationship. Though her thoughts had taken but a few seconds, she seemed to have been standing there for an age.

He peered at her over his replenished fork. 'Maria. Are you ill? I asked if you slept well last night.'

'Oh, yes. Yes, I slept very well thank you,' she stammered. 'Why do you ask?'

She had to await his reply, while his fork deposited another large portion into the cavern of that massive frame.

'Sorry, my dear, but one must stoke the old engine you know. Let me see, where were we? Ah yes, I remember, I asked because when you came in just now, you looked decidedly off colour.'

At that moment Mrs Clements entered

the room, bearing a tray containing Maria's breakfast. 'Good morning. Merciful heavens, I shall never be able to eat all that food,' cried Maria, staring aghast at the piled up plate.

'Nonsense ma'am. This is just what you need before a long ride.'

★ ★ ★

Thomas seemed to have shrugged off all the traumatic revelation of the last two days, for his demeanour and his conversation were quite normal on their return journey.

Even so, within half an hour of entering Mount Pleasant, he went up to their room and moved the majority of his clothes to another room.

Annie happened to meet him on the landing, and came rushing downstairs to inform Maria. 'I just saw Master Thomas coming out of your room, carrying a pile of his clothes, and take them through another door further along the landing. 'What is wrong, Maria? What happened at Watersmeet?'

'Just about everything that could go wrong, did so,' she replied sadly. 'I will tell you all about it tomorrow when the men have gone to the yard.'

So Annie had to curb her curiosity until the following morning, when Maria took her to the library and, after making sure all the windows and the door were securely closed, she told her companion the whole sorry story.

Annie listened avidly with few interruptions, her face a picture of incredulity, until Maria had brought her up to date with this latest family crisis, and finally finished speaking.

Annie rose from her chair and poured each of them another glass of sherry. 'Well, I'll be damned!' she said heatedly. 'Do you mean to tell me, he actually believes he had a visitation from poor Kate in his stupid dream?'

'Absolutely.' Maria replied, pausing to take a sip of her sherry. 'Though we must not blame him unduly Annie. As you will agree he had a terrible experience finding that damn snuff box at Miles's wedding.'

'Yes, now that's another thing,' interposed Annie. 'Imagine a lovely girl like Ruth, turning out to be the daughter of Charlie Butler, and dear sweet Aunt Lottie, Charlie's mother. Heavens, what a revelation. It all seems so incredible Maria.'

'Yes I know dear, but you must not breathe a word of this to anyone Annie, not even to your husband. Thomas has suffered too much already, and it would break my heart to see him further humiliated by some innocuous remark from an acquaintance at the yard.'

'Of course Maria. As you well know, I am not in the habit of spreading gossip. Anyway, how long is this separate bedroom farce going to last?'

Maria sighed. 'I really don't know, dear,' she replied wistfully. 'I can only hope and pray that time will erode and eventually destroy this phantom Kate of his dream, and we can then continue to live in harmony.'

* * *

A sun-tanned Miles and a happy contented Ruth, returned from their honeymoon in Italy at the end of the month, flushed with a sense of euphoria and well being, after their first taste of married bliss.

Lucy had invited the young couple to live with her at The Gables, for as long as they wished, providing Thomas and Maria agreed, which of course they did immediately. For Thomas had made it very clear in most explicit language, that in no circumstance would he ever live under the same roof as 'that mass murderer's daughter!'

The adoration with which Miles treated

his lovely new bride, both in public and in private, soon began to show in a more physical way, for nine months and one week after the day of their wedding, Ruth presented him with a fine baby boy, who was later christened Alan.

A new baby suddenly appearing within the confines of a family circle, can sometimes prove to be a wonderful catalyst, in promoting a sea change in the attitudes of some members of that family towards their kith and kin, and this is exactly what happened to Thomas. For, when Ruth's baby was one month old, Maria had finally persuaded Thomas to take her along to The Gables, to see their first grandchild.

Miles, Ruth and Lucy were thrilled to see Thomas arrive, as this was the first time he had called since the wedding, and none of them could understand why he had stayed away so long, for of course they had no inkling of the real cause of his prolonged absence.

However, as the afternoon progressed, Maria watched with a mounting feeling of happiness and better times ahead, as Thomas became more and more relaxed, and obviously enjoyed the intelligent conversation of his beautiful daughter-in-law. Then Maria's cup of happiness was filled to the brim. For

Ruth suddenly, and without warning, thrust her baby into the arms of his grandfather.

'There you are father. You hold him for a while. I am sure your arms are so much stronger than mine.'

Thomas was caught completely unawares, and at first seemed embarrassed by this tiny bundle lying so peacefully in the crook of his arm, but then Maria sighed with relief as she saw his countenance soften, and a new light of tenderness shine from those normally brilliant blue eyes, which had lain dormant for so many months.

'There you are darling. This is your grandpapa,' cooed Ruth, whose womanly intuition had warned her that for some inexplicable reason Miles's father hadn't been over friendly towards her since the day of the wedding, but now she was determined to win back his affection, even if she had to use her baby son as a means to that end.

'Oh Miles, don't they make a lovely picture?' trilled Ruth ecstatically to her husband, as he sat quietly enjoying what was to him this new rather unusual domestic scene.

'Yes indeed. Now be careful you don't drop him father.'

'Drop him!' echoed Thomas. 'Let me tell you something you young whippersnapper,

I wish I had as many sovereigns in my pocket as times I have cradled you in my arms like this.'

'I think you would find it rather difficult to cradle him now, Thomas,' quipped a delighted Maria.

On the way home that evening, Thomas was in an exuberant mood, and full of animated conversation about his plans for young Alan, and how he would train him to become a Master shipbuilder, to carry forward the name of Cartwright into the next century.

To Maria's surprise, immediately after supper that night, Thomas asked to be excused, saying he was feeling rather tired and wished to retire early.

However, Maria, Annie and Bull continued talking for some considerable time after he had gone, and another hour had elapsed, before Maria finally dragged herself upstairs to her lonely room.

As she entered, the lamp was turned low, though there was still sufficient light for her to undress, so without looking at the bed she removed all her clothes, for the night was warm, and pulling down a corner of the covers, she jumped into bed.

'Good evening,' said the voice, which for so many years had never ceased to thrill her.

'Nice of you to join me.'

'*Thomas!*' shrieked Maria, as she became engulfed in those beloved, familiar arms, and all those months of lonely sleepless nights, were swept away in one unforgettable glorious night of love.

His absence from their bed was never mentioned, nor did he ever speak of that ghastly, horrendous weekend they spent together at Watersmeet, or the subsequent damning discoveries he had unearthed from the church records. And for all of this, Maria was truly thankful.

During the following four years, Ruth gave birth to three more children. Two boys, and then a much wanted daughter, and they were christened, first Alan, then Brian, Charles and finally Debbie.

After the christening of the fourth child, Maria discreetly drew Miles to one side, away from the rest of the family. 'What is it, mother?' he asked, a trifle impatiently, wishing to return and bathe in the reflected glory of this latest addition to his brood.

Maria, as was her wont, came straight to the point. 'Tell me Miles. Do you intend to go through the entire alphabet?'

'Whatever do you mean mother?' he asked, astonished by her question.

'*Well, you already have A, B, C, and D. I*

was wondering, will the last one be Zacharrias or Zoe?'

Miles creased up with laughter. 'Oh mother,' he gasped. 'It isn't very often you're funny, but when you are, you're hilarious,' he managed to say, as he collapsed in another fit of uncontrollable laughter. Gradually however, his mirth subsided, when he realised his mother was not even smiling.

'I must tell you, Miles, if you carry on like this, you will undoubtedly kill that wife of yours. You already have a surfeit of children, and any more could irretrievably damage her health.'

Miles finally realised she was serious. 'I think you are exaggerating a little mother, though I do worry about her, but what can I do? I only have to hang my pants on the end of the bed, and Ruth seems to get pregnant again.'

'I see,' remarked Maria thoughtfully. 'I think I had better have a word with your Ruth.'

'A word? What do you mean, have a word with her?'

Maria smiled knowingly. 'Ah, that is for me to know my son, and for you to discover later, from your loving wife. Please ask Ruth to join me, so we may have our little tête-à-tête.'

So Maria had her 'word' with her daughter-in-law, and was enraptured to discover, as Ruth so blushingly revealed, that all this loving and romping around in the marital bed was not entirely of her making.

This quite unexpected revelation did much to pleasurably massage Maria's ego. For she discovered that, because of his years of self imposed abstinence, her beloved Miles was a regular tiger between the sheets, and though the poor girl was terrified of yet another pregnancy, she did her best to satisfy the every whim of this husband, whom she so obviously adored.

However, after this short discussion with her mother-in-law, Miles's sex drive was considerably curbed, and no more little Cartwrights appeared on the scene. Consequently, a very thankful Ruth, quickly and miraculously assumed her youthful lissom figure, confidence and poise.

As the children grew older, Thomas and Maria would often ride over during the long summer months, and he and Miles would play cricket with the boys on the long sweeping lawns of The Gables, while Lucy and Maria would sit on the terrace and talk for hours, or play with Debbie and her dolls.

These halcyon days and evenings provided

Maria with some of the happiest memories of her life, until one particularly warm evening in late September when Alan had attained the age of fourteen. Being a big strong lad for his age, he had been elected to bowl.

The two women were relaxing in deck chairs at a safe distance from the pitch, sipping cool lemonade while watching the cricket. Thomas was batting, and his grandson sent down a fast good length delivery, which he just touched with his bat, sending the ball skimming away over the short grass.

'Oh! well played,' cried Lucy and Maria, at the same time putting their hands together and applauding this unexpected flash of skill, from one who was no longer a young man.

He began to run, while Charlie tore after the fast disappearing ball like a young greyhound. One run, two runs, and the onlookers, who included several members of Lucy's domestic staff, were all cheering Thomas as he set off for his third. Halfway down the pitch he suddenly faltered, stumbled and then, almost it seemed in slow motion, he collapsed like an ox felled by the slaughterman's hammer!

Maria's hand flew to her mouth as she screamed. 'Thomas!' She and Lucy ran as fast as they could towards the prostrate figure, while Charlie, hearing Maria's scream, had turned and forgetting the ball, was streaking back again to the pitch.

Alan however, was the first to reach his grandfather, and when Maria and Lucy arrived, he lifted his tear filled eyes, and announced in an amazed strangled whisper. 'He is dead. My grandfather is dead!'

'No! Dear God No!' cried Maria, as she struggled to turn the huge bulk of the man she loved. At last, with help from the others, Thomas was lying on his back. Maria gasped when she saw the pallor of his face, and angrily brushing away the blinding salt laden tears, she ripped open the front of his shirt and thrust her small hand inside, searching frantically for the slightest movement of his heart within the caverns of that massive chest, while Lucy despatched one of the gardeners to bring the pig cratch.

Suddenly Maria shrieked with joy. *'He is alive! My Thomas is alive. I just felt a faint heart beat. Thank God!'* and she fell forward, almost collapsing on top of the still body of her lover.

Miles bent down, and placing a hand beneath her arm gently lifted his mother to her feet. 'Come along mother,' he said tenderly. 'Father will be all right when we get him indoors.'

At that moment the gardener appeared,

pushing a long wooden contraption with two small wheels at one end and two short legs at the other, complemented by two extended handles for the purpose of lifting the legs clear of the ground, thus enabling a man to push the cratch along.

Normally of course, this strange looking vehicle was used to carry a pig after it had been slaughtered, and lowered from the tripod, but in the event proved ideal as a substitute for a stretcher.

The combined efforts of Alan, his brothers and the gardener, were required to lift the two and a half hundredweight body of the unconscious Thomas onto the cratch. Even then they could only move it along by Alan taking one handle and the gardener the other.

Meanwhile Lucy had sent a young stable lad on a fast horse to summon the doctor, and by the time the rest of them had struggled and sweated to manoeuvre the pig cratch with its human load up the steps, down the hall and into the drawing room, then with a final concerted effort, deposit Thomas carefully upon the sofa, the lad had returned with the doctor following closely behind.

Before the examination was complete, Thomas had regained consciousness and, when the doctor was leaving, Maria walked with him to his trap. He was their regular doctor and a firm family friend. He was also a man of vast experience, and had spent many years among the misery and degradation in the slums of Hull.

Because of his early medical background, Dr Henry Pullover was years ahead of many of his better educated and more sophisticated colleagues. For he had witnessed at first hand the hopelessness and the malnutrition of the poor, and the extravagant excesses of the rich.

Having seen the frailties of the human race at opposing ends of the social spectrum, he would often draw upon his wealth of experience and expound his futuristic theories, not only to his contemporaries, but also to some of his well-heeled, rather portly Victorian patients. These generally treated his remarks with a kind of dignified amusement and, though they thought him somewhat eccentric, continued to tolerate him, for they all knew there was no finer doctor in the county.

'Now look here, Maria,' began the small sprightly doctor as they reached the drive. 'Thomas has just suffered a slight heart attack.' He placed a conciliatory hand upon her arm as her step faltered, and his voice softened as he watched the colour drain from her face.

'I am dreadfully sorry, my dear. To speak to you in that manner was unforgivable, but you see I am trying to stress the point that your Thomas is far too heavy. Have you any idea how much he weighs Maria?'

'Yes,' she replied haltingly. 'As a matter of fact he was weighed only last week on a set of scales in the granary, and he just touched twenty two and a half stone.'

'Umm. Just as I thought. You are feeding him far too well, Maria.'

'Well I always provide a good table, but you know, Henry, a man of his stature is bound to demand more than an average person.'

'Yes, yes, I agree. Though as you are aware, I worked in the slums of Hull for some years, and never had a patient die of a stroke or a heart attack, though I had scores die through the lack of good nourishment, and disease from living in such appalling conditions. Tell me Maria. How many pigs do you kill each year?'

Maria was rather surprised by the doctor's remarks, and particularly by his last question. However she knew something of his reputation, and as so many others had before her, decided to humour him. 'Three, and occasionally four, depending on their weight at the time,' she replied.

'Ah, depending on their weight. What would you say the average weight might be?'

'Approximately thirty stone.'

Henry did a quick mental calculation. 'Thirty stone!' he echoed. 'My word, Maria. That means your family consumes about six tons of pig meat per annum.'

'Not quite, we give about half of each pig away you know.'

'Yes, my dear, I realise that, but that still leaves an awful amount of meat for one family, along with the game and poultry, not forgetting the odd bullock and sheep or two.'

Maria was beginning to feel distressed at the trend this conversation was taking, and she had the distinct impression the doctor was surreptitiously inferring, her beloved Thomas was some kind of glutton.

'Yes, I suppose it is, but Mr and Mrs Hyde sit down at the table with us you know, and he can dispose of a fair amount at one sitting, plus the fact that we have lots of guests and shooting parties throughout the season,' she replied, determined to eradicate this slur upon her lover.

'Oh, yes, my dear, I agree,' said the

doctor placatingly, for he could see Maria was becoming annoyed. 'However, taking all that into account, Thomas is still far too heavy, and I am quite serious now, Maria. If you wish to prolong his life, you must somehow persuade him to curtail his voracious appetite, and I insist that he loses four or possibly five stone within the next twelve months, otherwise I cannot accept responsibility for any recurrence of today's happening. Please remember, my dear, the next one could be fatal!'

Maria clutched the arm of her friend. 'But Henry, what can I do if he refuses to comply with your instructions? You know how he enjoys his food.'

As the doctor looked at this still beautiful woman, he saw the tears in those lovely violet eyes, and his heart went out to her, for he knew how desperately she loved Thomas Cartwright, and it was at times like this he despised himself and his profession.

'Yes, Maria I do, and it will be very difficult for you both,' he replied softly. 'You must explain the situation to him. Be as blunt and frank as you can, so that you shock him into the full realisation of what will happen if he continues his present lifestyle and, when he goes shooting, encourage him to walk more and ride less. A couple of miles a day, would do you both a world of good.'

'A couple of miles a day!' repeated Maria incredulously. 'But Henry, exercise such as walking will only serve to increase his appetite and therefore exacerbate the problem.'

Henry smiled. 'Indeed it might, and in case that happens, take one or two apples along with you. They should help to placate any pangs of hunger he may experience.' With one foot upon the step of his trap, the doctor turned. 'Please do not worry unduly, Maria. Thomas has the constitution of an ox, and with a little help and encouragement from you, could well live for another twenty years.'

He hoisted himself up into his trap. 'I will look in again tomorrow,' he said as he took hold of the reins. 'Oh and just one more thing. Please tell him, Maria. No more cricket!'

After the doctor had left, Maria stood for some moments deep in thought, wondering how she could persuade Thomas to cope with all the instructions thrust upon her by the professional harbinger of doom and gloom.

At last she turned and, with a sigh and a muttered 'Take a couple of apples along!' followed by a short bitter laugh, she entered the house.

Maria halted in front of a mirror in the hall, and wiped her eyes to remove any trace of the tears she had shed whilst talking to the doctor. After a last grimace at herself she endeavoured to assume a happier, less doleful appearance to present to the world, as she proceeded down the hall to the drawing room door.

'Ah, here's mother now,' announced Miles, as Maria opened the door and walked in. He was standing by the window. Thomas and Ruth were seated upon the sofa, and Lucy was reclining, somewhat nonchalantly, in a large easy chair.

All of this flashed across Maria's vision in the twinkling of an eye, as her gaze became riveted upon the man she loved.

'Oh, my darling,' she cried, her voice filled with relief and happiness. 'It is so wonderful to see you sitting up. How do you feel now, my dear?' she asked, perching herself next to him upon the arm of the sofa, and reaching for his hand.

'Much better than I did half an hour ago I can assure you, though I am beginning to feel rather hungry.' His grip tightened upon her hand as he watched her countenance change, and her lovely eyes fill with sadness. 'What is it, Maria? What did Henry tell you out there?'

Maria hesitated, while she allowed her gaze to flit around the room: on their son standing by the window; the others seated on the sofa and chair, all of them tense, and waiting to hear what she had to say.

In as few words as possible, Maria gave the man she loved a summary of what the doctor had said. 'So you see my dear, if you wish for a long life, you will simply have to eat less,' she ended with a tremulous smile.

There was complete silence in the room after she finished speaking and, though Maria had expected an explosion of invective from Thomas, none came, and at last he spoke.

'I see,' he said softly. 'Well old Henry is a damn good doctor, so we must assume he knows what he is talking about. So the way I see it, I either die of hunger or a fatted heart. However, I will go along with this punishment, providing you help me, Maria. Yes, perhaps I could afford to lose four or five stone during the next twelve months.'

Maria flung her arms around his neck. 'Oh, you dear, dear man. I was so afraid you would take umbrage at what Henry said. Of course I will do all I can to help, but ultimately it must be your decision to continually refuse those second helpings, which you invariably ask for.'

He pretended to appear miserable and forlorn, then quite unexpectedly he kissed her, while Miles and Ruth looked on in embarrassed amusement, and Lucy a trifle enviously, as she saw the depth of love these two shared. Then, discreetly, the three of them withdrew.

So the great thinning of Thomas Cartwright began and, after four months of stringent compliance with the doctor's demands, he had to replace the entire contents of his wardrobe, with the exception of his socks, shoes and hats. He had to admit however, that he felt much fitter and, after the scheduled twelve months had expired, he declared the time had come for him to return to the yard.

Because of the decline of the whaling industry, and the consequent scarcity of whale oil, other sources had to be found, and finally the linseed and other oils were extracted by more and larger mills. Following these came flour milling, cement and paint, in addition to which, the ship building continued to grow, and the town of Hull increased in size beyond all recognition from the way Thomas remembered it when a boy.

The old narrow streets were totally inadequate to deal with the ever growing stream of traffic, and huge quantities of old buildings were demolished, to make way for fine, wide streets, lined with shops and public buildings. Then came the tram lines and horse drawn trams, the horses to be replaced later with electric power.

All these inventions and alterations, as the country headed toward the next century, coupled with the fact that everyone in the town seemed to be in a hurry, proved too much for Thomas and, after another five years of unstinting service to the yard of Earnshaw and Cartwright, he finally decided to hand over total control to Miles.

The next few years passed uneventfully for Thomas and Maria, though there were a couple of highlights, when they attended the weddings of two of their grandsons, Alan and Brian. Otherwise, Thomas spent much of his time adding to his superb collection of model ships, ingeniously placed into seemingly ridiculously small, though sometimes extravagantly shaped bottles.

However, when Thomas was in his eightieth year, the Grim Reaper called once again to stalk the inmates of Mount Pleasant, and he was inconsolable when two men brought in the body of Bull Hyde, who had apparently collapsed and died whilst walking within the confines of the garden.

Six months later, Thomas and Maria were just coming to terms with the loss of their life long friend, when one of the maids discovered the body of Annie in her bed. She had seemingly died peacefully in her sleep.

Maria was totally devastated by Annie's death, for she had been her friend, companion and confidante for more than half a century. In fact, ever since she had been taken to the cottage to live with Thomas, all those years ago.

The passing of their closest friends, one following so quickly after the other, had a profound effect upon the life of Thomas, and recently Maria had occasionally walked into the library and found him gazing up at William's favourite picture of that panoramic view, of the confluence of the three rivers below Watersmeet.

Unknown to her, Thomas had for some weeks been experiencing the same dream over and over again, when he would be walking along that same foreshore, and see the phantom like figure of his beloved Kate floating towards him and yet, run as he might, he never seemed to get any closer to her.

One crisp morning in early Spring, Maria

was surprised when he joined her at the breakfast table, because for several months she had breakfasted alone, as Thomas had taken to rising late.

'Good morning, Maria,' he greeted her warmly.

She looked at him keenly. Something had happened to put him in such an ebullient mood as this. 'What is wrong? Couldn't you sleep this morning?'

'I had no desire to Maria. We are leaving this old pile, and moving on to something smaller and more compact.'

Maria carefully set down her cup, then patted her mouth with a table napkin, before raising her head and looking him straight in the eye. 'Moving on Thomas? Whatever do you mean?' she asked quietly, though she thought she was about to hear the words she had been expecting, and dreading for months.

'Well, my dear, I mean this house is far too big for us now, and just think of the army of servants and gardeners we employ, to attend upon our meagre needs. Anyway, I have decided to hand the place over to Alan. He has two children of his own now, and June is expecting her third, I'm sure they will appreciate the room there is here. They must almost be living in each other's pockets over at The Gables.'

'Why don't you come right out with it Thomas and tell me where we are going, instead of all this shilly-shallying.'

His old eyes crinkled with amusement as he smiled at her. 'You always were a shrewd one, Maria. I bet you already know what I'm about to say. Perhaps you would care to tell me?'

'I can do that in one word. Watersmeet!' she snapped.

Though he had suspected she knew, he was still rather taken aback. 'How did you guess, my dear?' he asked.

'Oh, you don't need to look so surprised, my dear Thomas. I have seen you often enough mooning over that landscape in the library with a far away look in your eyes, so I have been expecting something like this for some time now.'

'Dear me, Maria. Is nothing sacred? You never fail to amaze me with your wonderful intuition, and your enviable capacity for love.'

Maria rose from her chair and kissed him. 'Why thank you, kind sir. What a marvellous way to start the day. You should get up at this time every morning,' she said, as she walked towards the door.

'Hey, wait a minute. What do you have

to say about us moving, and where are you going?'

Slowly she turned her head, and allowed her still lovely violet eyes to wash over him. 'Why? Do I have a choice, Master Thomas?' she quipped. 'I was just on my way to organise some of the packing for this move of ours. Anyway, you should know by now that where thou goest, so shall I, and there shall I be buried.'

Before he could think of a suitable reply, the door had closed softly behind her.

One month later, Thomas and Maria were installed in the three storey house at Watersmeet and, during the first day there, he called Maria to come upstairs to the room at the top. She entered the room, more than a little breathless from her climb, and more than a little irritated after the long drive from Hull.

'What is it, Thomas?' she gasped, as she flopped down on the edge of the bed.

'The trees, Maria!' he shouted, pointing out the window. 'Just look how those damn trees have grown. Another few years and it will be impossible to see the river, never mind the foreshore.'

For a moment Maria stared at him blankly, then her eyes briefly showed some of her old fighting spirit. 'You silly old fool!' she shouted. 'Do you mean you had me drag myself all the way up here, just to look at some stupid trees?'

Suddenly her features changed, and she laughed.

'What the devil are you laughing at?' he thundered.

Wiping her eyes with a tiny handkerchief, Maria struggled to compose herself. 'You said that in another few years it will be impossible to see the river darling. I was just wondering, how many more years do you intend to live?'

So Maria, though she hated having to climb all those stairs, stoically accepted them as part of the cross she had to bear for her great love of this man to whom she had given a lifetime of selfless devotion, but apart from the punishing climb, she really loved living at Watersmeet.

Maria adored the peaceful tranquillity of the village, the friendly uncomplicated lifestyle of the village people, the walks she and Thomas would take along the hill top path, and the hours they would sit by the maze and breathe in the magic of that panoramic enchanting scene. With the confluence of the three famous rivers, and the boundless acres of Yorkshire, stretching away into the distance, as far as the eye could see.

It was on one such occasion, when these two old friends and lovers for so many years, were sitting there enjoying the warmth of a late Spring sun, that Miles and Ruth found them, along with their two youngest children, Charles and Debbie.

Of course they were not children now, for Charles had recently celebrated his twentieth birthday, and his sister was well into her teens. However, Ruth still looked upon them as her young children.

'Hello grandpa,' cried Debbie, rushing up to Thomas and almost smothering him with kisses, then repeating the performance with 'Grandmama.'

'Look, Charles. Here's that wonderful maze that everyone has told us so much about. Do come along and let's try to solve it.'

After speaking to Thomas and Maria for a little while, the placid, dutiful Charles followed his more exuberant sister into the realms of what, until now, he had always looked upon as some kind of fantasy or legend dreamt up by his grandparents, then handed down over the years to his parents.

However, they had a thoroughly enjoyable time, and when they flung themselves, hot and flustered, upon the grass beside the others, they vowed to bring Alan's children the next time they visited Watersmeet.

Epilogue

With the passing of time, birthdays and Christmas seemed to come round much more quickly for Thomas and Maria, and now he had been confined to his room at the top of High House for more years than he could remember, but Maria never complained. She would go up to sit with him for an hour each morning, then again in the evening, to ensure he was in his bed at night.

Often, when she entered the room, he would be sitting before the window in his well worn leather chair, scanning the distant foreshore through his precious telescope. Though Maria knew for what he was searching, she never reproached or upbraided him.

It was on a warm evening during late summer, when Maria entered that room for the last time. He was lying back in his chair, as if he was sleeping, his telescope resting upon the windowsill, yet immediately Maria entered the room, she clutched her breast. For she knew that Thomas Cartwright, this wonderful man whom she had worshipped all her adult life, had at last gone to join his beloved Kate.

With a strangled cry of. *'My darling Thomas,'* Maria stumbled forward, and kissed the stiff pale lips, as she stroked the cold marble of his face.

'Please forgive me darling,' she muttered brokenly. 'I should have been with you, to say goodbye.'

Eventually, Maria sank to the floor, and with choking heartrending sobs, she wrapped her arms around the stiff cold legs of the man she had loved more than life itself.

Never knowing how many hours she clung to her dead lover, finally, through sheer exhaustion, Maria dragged herself across the room and, using the last ounce of her failing strength, she managed to pull up her frail and tired body, to lie gasping and sobbing upon his bed.

★ ★ ★

The village of Watersmeet was once more awash beneath a sea of sombre black, for this was a double funeral, and the streets were filled with black coaches, black horses proudly bearing quivering plumes of black ostrich feathers, and hundreds of people all wearing black.

Miles was sure he had detected just the hint of a smile upon his mother's lifeless lips. Though of course he could not even begin to guess the reason for this unusual phenomenon.

Maria had known for some time the churchyard was full, and that a new cemetery had been opened on the outskirts of the village and, when the time came, she and her lover would be laid to rest side by side. *So that in death as in life, they would forever be together.*

We do hope that you have enjoyed reading this large print book.

Did you know that all of our titles are available for purchase?

We publish a wide range of high quality large print books including:
Romances, Mysteries, Classics, General Fiction, Non Fiction and Westerns.

Special interest titles available in large print are:
The Little Oxford Dictionary
Music Book
Song Book
Hymn Book
Service Book

Also available from us courtesy of Oxford University Press:
Young Readers' Dictionary
(large print edition)
Young Readers' Thesaurus
(large print edition)

For further information or a free brochure, please contact us at:
Ulverscroft Large Print Books Ltd.,
The Green, Bradgate Road, Anstey,
Leicester, LE7 7FU, England.
Tel: (00 44) **0116 236 4325**
Fax: (00 44) **0116 234 0205**

Other books in the
Ulverscroft Large Print Series:

LAND OF MY DREAMS

Kate North

Maisie, an elderly lady, has lived in the shadow of her domineering and reclusive mother. Now her mother is dead and Maisie finally has a chance at life — one she comes to see and to experience through her new neighbours, the recently bereaved Clare and her teenage son, Joe. The unlikeliest of friendships begins as Joe, acting almost instinctively, draws Maisie out of her shell. Gradually, the secret that kept Maisie and her mother on the move and away from society is revealed, and Maisie finds the strength to make one last bid for happiness.